The Smallest of Entryways

Dear Megan,

I hope you enjoy

by Cristen Hemingway Jaynes

these stories — some of
them are set in our
old neighborhood!

Love,

♡ Cristen

Artwork: "Kitchen Drawers" by Amelia Santiago,
used with permission.

SECOND AMERICAN EDITION
ISBN: 978-0-9973456-0-5

Church Row Books, Brooklyn NY

First Edition Copyright © 2012 Cristen Hemingway Jaynes,
ISBN: 978-0-635-73360-9

chum literary publishing, Brooklyn, NY

Library of Congress Cataloging-in-Publication Data
Jaynes, Cristen Hemingway [1972]
The Smallest of Entryways
Short Stories; Collection [2001-2012]

There are two candles;
one in the window, for hope,
the other lit for mourning.

CONTENTS

INTRODUCTION

As a writer I've always thought that credit should be given where credit is due, and that whenever you encounter another writer who has what it takes to leave something to the world that should be read and read again, then it's a gift to everyone. You can never be jealous of another writer who writes well. If anything we need to celebrate the fact that in an age of global barbarities and cultural decline there are still artists who are not afraid to remind us of our own shared humanity.

"Chapeau" is an expression that often came to mind when I was reading Cristen Hemingway Jaynes' short story collection, *The Smallest of Entryways*. I didn't expect to catch myself saying it as often as I did, but, as I said before, credit needs to be given where credit is due. Many of her tales are from the point of view of children, such as 'The Laundromat' and 'Vienna Sausages'. They are stories of innocence and cross-country trips that are at the same time very descriptive and nuanced and yet haunting. In 'The Laundromat', a divorced mother and her young daughter are having dinner at a McDonald's. The restaurant and its bright colors are, as the author reminds us, a place of refuge and comfort.

"Now that he was gone these people were comforting. It was a kinship of many kinds of desperation; at the very least they had not had enough time or endurance to make dinner for themselves or their families and had given in, relenting in the face of difficulty, taking comfort in meat, oil, and sugar."

But the McDonald's is also a reflection of the desolation of America, a sterile, cold reminder of what we've become, "The mother watched the fryers. For some reason her stare, the nervous stare of waiting, was always taken back to the fryers. When they dumped the new batch of finished fries into the metal holding container, hot from the oil, she pulled her daughter close to her side, hugging her tight."

In '100 Years from Now', the language used and the brevity of the story together with its unspoken themes reminded me of the author's great-grandfather, Ernest Hemingway, and the ability that he had to put an idea in a reader's head almost without ever having to mention it. While in the last short story, 'The Smallest of Entryways', the author uses a stream of consciousness style that reminded me of Jewel Brundren's character in Faulkner's *As I Lay Dying*. It was hard to follow at first, but as soon as I let the flow of the words take over and I stopped trying to determine whether or not the narrator was insane, it made sense in a strangely beautiful, somewhat surreal, Florida Keys kind of way.

Knowingly or not, the author has paid homage to two of the greatest American writers of the last century, but like any good writer she remains rooted in her own time and tells us things about the present that most of us suspect, but that perhaps many of us don't want to see.

John Hemingway,
25 September 2015, Montreal

The Smallest of Entryways

1

THE LAMP

The drizzle covered the city in a stovepipe mist, tinting the grey concrete of the roads and buildings a bluish color. The father drove the old brown Rover that was new to him with the steady uncertainty of training a new horse. It was two o'clock, the first time he had come to the house since he'd moved out. He was there to pick up his daughter. The neighborhood was always quiet, its residents mostly old couples and widowed old women. The young couple and their daughter had ended up there thanks to the funeral home which they had lived above before buying the house. A few times the owner of the funeral home had asked the father to work for him, and though he had always said, "No, I have a job; thank you anyway," he had, a number of times, helped the owner if the owner found him at home. Sometimes the owner would knock on the apartment door if he saw the father's motorcycle, or if he saw him out in the yard of the funeral home playing with his daughter.

"Got a job," he'd say.

"Sure, give me a minute."

It was a quick fifteen dollars. At first it had bothered the father significantly, though he had tried not to let it. "It's just heavy lifting," he had told himself. "It happens to everyone." But it was just that, the weight of the bodies, that had bothered him.

The father went on a job with the owner of the funeral home one day to a house that was practically in the same neighborhood where they lived. The widow had died in her house and she had lived alone. There was still old coffee on the stove. She had died in her sleep, they'd said. They had found her body in bed. "No relatives," the owner of the funeral home said.

The father inquired and found that the house was for sale, and for much less than it was worth. He had a job at Levitz furniture and had managed to save money by putting it in a bean can under the kitchen counter.

When he and his wife went to look at the house, everything was the same as the day he had gone to get the body. The house had not been aired out all winter and the sunlight that came through the windows showed the particles in the air. It made the wife think of looking through the rum bottle she had dived down with to the sea floor in Bimini and filled with sea water thick with tiny shells and pieces of coral. The house was snug with antiques from the 1920s; in every drawer of the bureau, secretary and foot-peddle sewing machine were artifacts from the old couple's lives. The heavy metal razor, coat buttons, trouser socks, and some pretty snazzy hats evidenced the old man. The coffee was still on the stove. This unnerved the wife, but she liked the house and all the furniture, so she decided not to let the situation bother her. She used the old woman's spices, her laundry soap, even her rosewood shampoo. They gave away the old woman's clothes, except for her panty hose, but kept the man's, which the father wore to work, funerals, and at various other times.

Today the father returned to the house, the setting of he and his wife's marriage, for the first time since they'd separated. He had been 19 when his daughter was born. Now he had an eight year old daughter and was getting divorced. He was only 27 and had already caused so much damage. But, he was here to get his daughter and to take her out to wade in the stream next to the Sound and to play ghost baseball like he had done in the mountains of North Carolina. He couldn't fathom how different he would be when she graduated from high school. He had thought about lying to her about how old he and her mother were so that she wouldn't make the same mistakes. He stood in the city grass next to the street staring at the house. It needed painting. He had painted it brown right after they bought it. He had never cleaned the gutters. He noticed the stained, thick-slatted blinds were down. He thought about he and his daughter tossing the Nerf football back and forth, and how when it had gotten caught and gashed in the apple tree, she had put a band-aid on it.

'It's two in the afternoon,' he thought. 'Why are the blinds down, Lauren?'

He had never seemed to himself to be a sentimental person, but as he mounted the wooden stairs that he had replaced himself, he felt something like sentiment, the joy and bitter devotion to a place and time.

"Lauren," he said loudly as he knocked, trying to look around the crimson cloth that covered the other side of the tiny rectangular windows.

He heard multiple locks, then the tinny sound of the old doorknob as his daughter opened the door.

"Chris, hi, sweetheart. Where's your mother?"

"She's in bed. She's sick."

"Oh." he came in. "She didn't tell me."

The house seemed empty, as though his daughter lived there alone. He thought of the widow.

"Where are we going today, Dad?"

"I thought we'd go hiking at the park and play some baseball. Where's your mother?" He could smell the polite smell of menthols.

"Dad, she's in bed."

"What do you mean, she's sick?"

"She's sick."

"Did she say with what?"

"No."

"How long has she been in bed?"

"Three days."

"Well, that's ridiculous. Has she been feeding you?"

"Yes. We've been eating sandwiches."

"Sandwiches. For dinner."

"Uh huh."

"Well, we'll go get you a hamburger."

He walked through the entryway to the kitchen, next to the tiny hallway that contained the doors to the bedrooms: "Lauren." He heard her cough through the closed door.

"Lauren?" He walked over and stood outside her door. He felt her listening.

"Yes?"

"Can I come in?"

"I'll talk to you when you get back."

"Okay." He leaned close to the door as though it were necessary to make her hear him; as though it made them closer. "We'll be back around 5:30."

"Get her some dinner."

"I will."

His daughter was sitting in the middle of the rough red brocade couch. He took her hand and led her through the living room as though leading her out of a store or museum.

The park was practically empty. He didn't know why, but when he had envisioned he and his daughter on their first outing alone in their broken state, he had envisioned them wading through the stream that ran along the beach of Puget Sound like they did in the summer. When they got there he realized that they probably shouldn't even play baseball. They sat in the car in the parking lot in front of the foot bridge that led over the railroad tracks.

"It's raining," he said. "I'm sorry." He felt guilty for the rain. "Do you want to go walk down to the beach for a minute? I have an umbrella in the trunk."

"Okay."

He took the black umbrella from the trunk and handed it to his daughter. She held it in front of her like she'd seen people do, but struggled to get it to stay open. He took it, latched it open for her, then handed it back.

"Dad, you'll get wet."

"That's okay, honey."

"I don't want you to get wet. You hold it."

He took it and bent down over her as they walked through the gravel that led to the metal stairs of the scaffolding-like footbridge. He had never come there without Lauren, and they had never come there without Christy.

His daughter's little shoes clunked against the steep stairs as she struggled to climb them. The stairs were slatted so that they could see through them to the ground and he wondered if she was scared. He had always carried her before. The uneven plip-plop-plip of the rain against the umbrella punctuated the sounds of their feet, creating a static-like sound in his brain.

Puget Sound appeared as they reached the platform that stood just above the trees, a salty lake-like creature, misty in the expectant calm of the aging afternoon. They stood facing East over the tracks. They knew from experience which way the train came.

Looking far out to where the shoreline bent and curved to the North, they saw that no train was coming.

"You said Mom's been sick for three days?"

"I guess. She says she's sick. She's been in bed."

"Has anybody come over?"

"No, and she won't let me have anybody over either. Mary hasn't even come over. She's the only person she'll talk to on the phone, besides you when you call … Megan said Mary said Mom drinks too much."

"Does she? Have you seen her?"

"Yes, she's always carrying a glass with something she gets from the bottle in the cabinet."

"Huh." He wanted to say, 'Well, don't you worry about Mom, she's going to be fine, I'll fix this,' but he couldn't force himself.

They stood on the metal platform, not a soul to be seen. The railroad track and the shoreline divided the freshwater and sea-fed Sound from the park, bright with daisies and grass and Evergreen trees that stood still in the shapeless winter day.

All he'd ever seen Lauren drink was Bud and Rainier. He couldn't imagine her drinking like that. She must be trying to show him.

"There's no train," his daughter said.

They both thought of the day the three of them had come to see the sunset and had watched a train come around the bend, snaking toward them along the shore – it seemed to take forever to get to them – and when it had gotten close it had begun to move the ground in long shakes that felt like tall waves beneath a boat, and she had gotten a little scared, so both her parents had put a hand on each of her shoulders, then her father had picked her up and they had stood close while the train barreled right under them, seeming to have picked up great speed when it suddenly got close enough for them to jump down onto it, which they all thought about doing, and in the great noise that was beneath them, that would have forced them to yell if they'd wanted to talk, he remembered thinking of Christmas, of snow covering everything, the rock wall, the Subaru, the tops and sides of the bent cattails around the pond, around the tiny farmhouse in the mountains of North Carolina. He remembered standing there with the train rushing beneath them deciding to buy Lauren a winter coat, which she already needed in September, and feeling definitely that he loved her and their daughter.

"Want to go get a hamburger?" the father asked.

"Sure."

When they got back he picked up the balled-up orange wrappers from the passenger side floor and carried them to the garbage can on the side of the house. His daughter let herself in with a key. The house seemed blessedly still, like a dead wren. The leaves surrounding it had been there for months, since before he'd left. They had turned into dark brown and black compost. He felt guilty for not having come over to clean them. He didn't really want to go inside.

His daughter had left the door open for him. When he pushed it open he smelled the humid smell of boiling thyme and coriander, Lauren's corned beef boiling on the stove. The built-in shelf above the fireplace and bookshelves held Christmas cards; he recognized the ones from his family, all with the North Star, Jesus and the manger scene, and the squirrel tail he had found in the yard after Rumpus tore apart the rest of what was a particularly bloody kill, one which was apparently too torn apart to present to them on the porch. What he didn't see was the lamp with the macramé shade his wife had made hanging in the corner next to the window. It had taken her from mid-summer until Christmas, and she had given it to him with a card that said, "To study by" because he had been accepted that spring to the University of Washington.

The pictures she had torn from art books of Botticelli nudes, that his mother had called "pornography" when she and his father had visited, still graced the puce walls, brown dripping stains decorating the spaces in between from all the humidity of rainy days and boiling water.

"Where's the lamp?" he said too quietly for anyone to hear. Lauren had sat for hours in the backyard in the summer and fall on a green and white chaise lounge, pulling and twisting the thick dread-like fibers, then moved inside to the chair by the fireplace, the rough red chair that matched the couch, in the long and cozy holiday months to finish it. He had liked that lampshade, the way it dotted the ceiling with mosaic shadows and lit up Christy's collection of plastic horses that stood on the tiers of the tapered corner bookshelf.

He heard Lauren in the kitchen talking to Christy. He walked through the living room and stood in the kitchen door frame.

Lauren took the lid off the pot and held it up, showing her daughter the condensation.

"Mom's teaching me how to make rain," she said.

The father saw the glass, a short unmistakable shape, of a kind he had never owned and had never seen in their house, on the kitchen table next to the stove. It looked strange on the plastic, orange-flowered table cloth.

"Where's the lamp?"

"What," Lauren said flatly, not like she didn't know what he was talking about.

"The macramé lamp."

"I threw it away."

He decided to stop there, that it was better to leave.

"I'll pick her up next Saturday."

"Sure," she said shortly.

He turned to go, then remembered his daughter, who came over and held his leg. As he walked toward the door, his daughter behind him, he felt as though he should be leaving something, a marker of some kind.

He got in the old, sturdy Rover with the rusted door and hood. It choked and shook him before it died. He pumped the gas pedal, then tried again. It cut on. He sat there, staring at the beaded up drops on the windshield. He looked up at the window where the lamp used to be.

"You can't avoid it," he thought, revving the engine to go up the hill. "It just comes after you."

2

THE LAUNDROMAT

The street was quiet. There were many cars going home for the night from work, their lights passing, coming at them, and passing again. It was quiet; not the quiet of being covered in snow, but the humming quiet of rhythmic constancy. The street was wet with light rain and it made the sidewalks a dark gray as they walked to the grocery store not far from their house. It was something they had never done before. The red car lights were fuzzy in the misty rain and as they approached N. 85th St., the little girl could see the Chinese restaurant with its red letter lights and they were fuzzy too, in the rain.

The little girl's mother held her hand now that they

were at the corner of Greenwood and N. 85th. The bank where they had an account was across the street, and they had just passed the antique shop, as well as the 1950s restaurant where her mother's best friend worked. Across Greenwood, on the corner, was another antique shop and across the street from that was a dance studio. The dance studio caused an empty feeling in the little girl, especially when it was rainy and cold because it was so large and empty. Next to the dance studio was the music store where she took clarinet lessons every Wednesday after school.

They were going to Lucky's. It was the same grocery store where they had gone ever since the little girl could remember. They had never walked there before. The little girl, her mother and her father had usually gone there together in her father's little yellow Fiat. Occasionally, the girl and her mother had gone by themselves after school, in the dark blue Volkswagen bug, but that was mostly when the girl had taken half days at Montessori, before she'd started kindergarten. Sometimes, her father had gone by himself with a list. But never before had any combination of them walked.

The girl and her mother crossed N. 85th in the rain with their black umbrella, her mother in a brown sweater that wasn't enough for the wet September weather, and the little girl in a yellow slicker. Her mother looked very pretty with her black hair in the rain, tamped down with moisture and a little bit frizzy.

"I have to go to the grocery store," her mother had said when they were still at home. "Do you want to walk?" The little girl hadn't answered and her mother had immediately gathered the little girl's coat and the umbrella.

The girl looked up at her mother. She felt that she looked different. That she held a woeful look. The girl had never seen her mother wear her face in this way for more than a few minutes. It had been there when her mother's own mother had gotten into the bad car accident, but then the more long-lasting expression her mother's face had taken on was that of worry. The severe down-turn of mouth that her mother now wore had in the past been saved for moments of deep concern, or moments of crying, but then had dissipated. Now her mouth had the look that it had always been this way.

They passed the Chinese restaurant and then the coin and stamp shop that the girl's friend Meghan's dad had taken them to one Saturday afternoon where the little girl had bought a penny from 1857 and an envelope full of stamps from around Thailand and Botswana. She kept the penny in her nightstand, what was really an old wooden record holder, behind her books. She had decided that the coin and stamp shop was the first place she would go when she was allowed to go places by herself.

The little girl and her mother were shielded from the rain by the awnings of the businesses. Across the street was the McDonald's. When she was a baby it had been a laundromat underneath which stray cats had lived. The three of them, the little girl, her mother and father, had gone there with sheets and pillowcases full of flannel shirts, denim short shorts, and baby clothes. One night they had gone home while the laundry was drying and all of it had been stolen. Her father had been quiet all the way home, then had gone to the porch to smoke a joint and gone to bed. The next day, he had called his parents and told them what had happened. They had sent baby clothes that were nicer than the clothes from the Salvation Army that the little girl had been wearing. They had then switched laundromats.

In the summer, they hadn't gone to the laundromat. The girl's mother and Mary, her best friend, had done the wash in the backyard with the old ringer washer that had been in the basement of the house when they had bought it. But when the little girl's mother had gone to the grocery store to get tea bags to make sun tea and had witnessed, as she was driving down N. 85th Street, the old white dirty wooden building being knocked down and pulled apart, its wood walls that had been the destination of their Saturday family outings splintering like kindling, the little girl's mother was distraught. The laundromat building seemed like a large, dried-out bug, a behemoth of the antediluvian world being hauled off to disintegrate, its significance soon to exist only in her memory.

There was a large puddle under one of the awnings of a bar and the girl and her mother stepped around it and the dripping water. The mother looked down at the girl's feet to check if they were getting too wet. "We should have put on your rain boots," she said. When they got to the parking lot of Lucky's her mother stopped in front of the corral of carts in front of the store. "I don't know how we're going to get all of the groceries back. I won't be able to hold the umbrella and the groceries at the same time." She kept her hand on the cart. She wished she could talk to her daughter sort of like a girlfriend, to at least be able to explain things. She wanted to tell her how the lady who had brought them muffins was not what she seemed. She had told her daughter it was okay when she'd looked up from the gooey, undercooked mess that the woman, another mother from the preschool, had brought to the picnic in a brown basket. "She's not so into berries," she had told the woman. She felt badly now for making excuses for her daughter. She felt guilty for encouraging her to eat something not up to par. The woman was not up to par, she thought. Men don't care, she wanted to tell her daughter. Sometimes, they just don't care.

Her daughter stood next to her, next to the grocery cart. The rain splashed against the metal of the cart, sometimes the big drops splashing onto their bare hands. The little girl thought about her dad. She thought how if he were there, there would be no questioning. They would go inside. They would get food. He would get her one of the donuts from the bakery counter to eat while they were shopping. She would sit under the cart and let him push her, though lately she had preferred to walk beside him while her mother put things into the cart.

"I think maybe we should go to McDonald's," her mother said. Her mother never took her to

McDonald's. The only time she ever got to eat at McDonald's was when her friend's parents took her. She often thought about the day when she could go to the stamp and coin shop and then afterward to McDonald's by herself.

"Maybe go in and just get some things for breakfast first," her mother said.

They went inside the grocery store and walked over to the cereal and breakfast aisle. There were a lot of breakfast foods that the little girl and her dad liked. He liked to get Grape Nuts and pancake mix and Mrs. Butterworth's syrup, while the little girl got Quaker Maple & Brown Sugar oatmeal and Carnation Breakfast Bars. The little girl's favorite part of going to the grocery store was standing with her father in front of the Carnation Breakfast Bars and talking about what kinds to get. He would ask her what flavors she was in the mood for and talk about how many combinations they had or tell her what sounded good to him. She had asked him why he didn't eat them and he had said they were too sweet. She made the point that he ate pancakes with syrup on them, but he said that was a special thing he reserved for himself for the weekends, which is when he went jogging, too, but if he ate Carnation Breakfast Bars he would probably eat them too often and then he would get fat. This had made her laugh. She couldn't imagine her father fat. He was thinner than any other dad she knew.

The little girl's mother didn't often eat breakfast. She put some oatmeal and Cream of Wheat, which she ate sometimes on the weekends on really cold days, into the cart.

The little girl stood in front of the Carnation Breakfast Bars. They were daunting. The last time she had gotten Peanut Butter Crunch. Her father never let her get the same flavor more than twice in a row. He said it wasn't good to be too much a creature of habit, only old people were allowed to eat the same things all the time. She already got the same thing every time at Guadalajara, the Mexican restaurant they went to. She couldn't see anything except Peanut Butter Crunch. She forced herself to read and process the meaning of another label. S'mores. Didn't sound good at all. She couldn't reach the Peanut Butter Crunch, it was on the top shelf.

She looked over at her mother. She was staring at the Grape Nuts.

"Mom. Can you get this down for me?"

It was still raining and the parking lot had a black oil-slickness as they shuffled out of the store with their one paper bag under the mother's arm.

They crossed the parking lot and went to the corner. The red "Don't Walk" light was flashing, so they waited, the little girl half under the umbrella, the hair that was sticking out from her hood getting wet. They both watched the traffic going by, small hydroplanes of water under the car tires making the sound of rushing water. Her mother looked over at the McDonald's. She thought how that one thing had changed the neighborhood, legitimizing and destroying it in some way, making it modern by taking away its origins.

The mother wondered if her daughter knew; if she knew that her mother was waiting. During the week, the little girl was used to her father getting home after she went to bed, and only seeing him sleeping through a crack in the door in the mornings when she got her tiny, heavy coat out of the hall closet. The little girl always looked in on her father through the crack. Recently, her mother had told her he was out of town. But the next weekend he was coming, and they would have to talk about it.

The mother tried to think about what it would be like to do things with her daughter on her own. They could make frozen chocolate bananas and leave them in the freezer until they'd eaten them all at their leisure, for a month if they liked. "He'll come over and look in the freezer," she thought. "He'll come over and look in the freezer to see if I'm doing okay, to see if I'm keeping the right things in there."

She thought about how it would have been just like any other relationship if they hadn't gotten married. The furniture they bought would still have come from the furniture store where he worked part-time to put himself through school and from Salvation Army. The pots and pans, the alfalfa sprout growing kit, the macramé lamps her best friend had made for them, the Botticellis torn from art books, the air heavy with greasy condensation that stuck to and dripped down the walls, all the same as it would have been if they hadn't married each other. But that they had gotten married made it sadder to her in some way. Their things had a life story that would change; where they had bought them, and when, just like if they had been bought in another relationship, but their being married and then one day not would draw a very stark line. Even if one or the other of them had bought them, they had bought them for each other, for their marriage. Everything was for their marriage. Everything was for each other. The story couldn't continue as though she had brought the tiny dresser or pair of wool pants from Salvation Army or the book, even, home one day for herself alone.

She had planted the sprouts one Sunday morning while he was asleep. The sun had shone on the foam green tiles flecked with yellow and red of the kitchen floor, and she had looked through the window filled in its frame with the bright yellow glow of forsythia blossoms, out at the apple and cherry trees of their yard, and had allowed herself to be engulfed by the daunting contented sleepwalk of married life. Her husband in the bedroom sleeping-in, her daughter, a baby then, sleeping, too, but about to wake, needing nothing but this womb of blown glass that was their home.

The mother didn't know if she and, consequently, the situation was the way that it was because the one thing her parents had said they'd agreed upon about raising her was that she be independent. She worried that their ideas about this had been so different that it had made her too independent, more independent than they'd ever wanted. She worried that it had just been an excuse for them not to have had to come to an agreement about how to raise their daughter, to decide what the right direction was. She felt that no guidance was misguidance. She felt that she had no direction.

She took her daughter's hand as they stepped off the curb to cross the evening street, the cars on either side of the crosswalk seeming like horses at the banks of a river. They turned left onto Greenwood Avenue N., passing another bank, a sub shop, the only shoe repair store she knew of anymore, a soul food restaurant, an Italian restaurant, a doughnut shop. Next to the doughnut shop was the McDonald's. It was brightly lit with people seated at the plastic booths eating fries and hamburgers, drinking sodas and milkshakes. She opened the door for her daughter. Her daughter looked up at her, but didn't say anything as she walked through the door.

The mother remembered that she liked McDonald's. She liked their little yellow papered cheeseburgers. She used to take her daughter and her friends there after preschool. She had stopped going because her husband had made her feel guilty about "feeding that shit to our daughter."

The large number of people eating quickly, with such clear purpose, made her grateful. The fluorescent lights, the beeping of the fryers being done, the sharp, "Anything else?"s had the familiarity of safety in numbers.

She stood in line with great gratitude, as though it were Christmas and she'd had nowhere to go. She looked down at her daughter, who was not looking up at the menu, but looking around at the big bodies flanking her like trees in a forest.

"Mom, I want a cheeseburger and Chicken McNuggets. If I don't finish the McNuggets, I can save them for later."

"Okay, sweetie. Do you want to share my fries? How about a milkshake or a Coke?"

"I'll have a chocolate shake, and I'll share your fries." She smiled up at her mother, and her mother realized that she hadn't seen her look that happy since dinner the past Sunday when her father had pretended to be the wind at the park, blowing her face and her hair while she closed her eyes and laughed. He had left that night after their daughter had gone to sleep.

They stood next to the counter waiting for their food. The mother thought of how the spot she was standing on used to be surrounded by round circle-faced machines kaleidoscopically turning their clothes around. The father used to stand outside smoking and looking at the people walking by, or would sit in one of the plastic chairs doing physics equations. The mother would stand in the alley of washers, watching their daughter wander around looking into the portholes at the clothes flipping and flopping around, looking deeply into the detergent machine slots and their contents, or standing in the doorway "with" her father while he smoked. Sometimes, they would dance; a sort of a waltz, slow and led by the father, who felt his daughter's little hands leaning into his, waiting to be shown by feel what to do next. The evening air had come in through the open front door, replacing some of the heat in the steamy box that the laundromat had become as their clothes tumbled through their cycles. There had not often been other people in the laundromat.

The mother looked around at all the people eating through the din of fast food. Now that he was gone these people were comforting. It was a kinship of many kinds of desperation; at the very least they had not had enough time or endurance to make dinner for themselves or their families and had given in, relenting in the face of difficulty, taking comfort in meat, oil, and sugar.

There they stood: where once had been a stone floor was now a stone floor painted white with cheap paint. Where once had been wood walls were now brightly clean windows with fluorescent lights' reflections. Where once were rows of machines designed to help better their lives were bright red and yellow images rising up like monuments. And, most heartbreaking, where once had been a dominion of cats beneath the wooden framework was now a wasteland, its edges dripping with water when it rained, no longer a shelter.

The mother watched the fryers. For some reason her stare, the nervous stare of waiting, was always taken back to the fryers. When they dumped the new batch of finished fries into the metal holding container, hot from the oil, she pulled her daughter close to her side, hugging her tight

3

VIENNA SAUSAGES

I looked upward through the defrost-capable glass of the Lima bean to the back heads of Lila and Tommy, the cigarette-lighter TV between them. I wished the puff of cloud would stay above us forever. We were driving between the fur trader hills and alongside the chapel window rivers of Montana. I hadn't seen a Motel 6 since Dispute, Idaho. Telephone poles were staked like fire lookouts on the horizon. I lay in the backseat, surrounded by pink bear, purple weirdo guy, a family of white bunnies with dresses and knickers, a chambray comforter and pillow. The inside of the car was like the inside of a submarine, everyone to their position. Sometimes Tommy and I would play hangman, but mostly it was me and the moving view.

My mother looked out the window. Early afternoons, when we first checked out of the last motel, the jokes were over. When evening came, I kept an eye out for the next Motel 6 or Super 8. Lit up space stations waiting for us to pull up and attach for refueling. Beds with appendages like pinball machines. I popped a quarter in, hopped onto the rayon and polyester, and was jarred around like a bean sorter. At noon, after our one-hour extension had expired, the housekeepers would kindly smile as they invaded our fox burrow, the rotary phone ringing its recess-bell-ring. The front desk egging us on our way, everyone clamoring in an effort to send us back into the world of pavement and dust.

Lila rolled down her window. The bellows-draft blew in a swarm of crows around her head. She sped off with them into the distance. Soldiering on, I lay back, content to never arrive. The checked boxes were done for what would have been third grade. That last day Lila had come to school to get me, she had seemed so tall and believable. The teacher had told her, nonchalantly, that, yes, they'd be expanding on things, going forward, but nothing she didn't think I could do with vigor and enthusiasm and speed, to say nothing of perfection, and as I had been called Brainiac by the other kids, and had taken unbelievable sportsman's enthusiasm at find-the-book-in-the-stacks in the school library, and had even hung out there during lunch, my friends and I making it our clubhouse, other nonbookenthusiast kids harassing us obscenely, accusing me of saying something derogatory about one of their mamas, the teacher thought it would be okay for me to go to a tropical island for the next year to see what I could learn.

The poles flicked by like matchsticks through the back window of the hatchback, filled past safety's brim with books, film canisters, fishing poles and things I knew not of because I didn't know what they kept in their drawers and closets.

"Honey, we'll be stopping in a minute. Think about what snacks you want to tide you over until dinner. They might have Vienna Sausages. You had them when we went fishing with your dad at the Kettle River, remember?"

I remembered dad filled with an enthusiastic outdoor quality, fresh air and mountain vigor. I was always stunned at mom's ability to tell stories involving dad in front of Tommy without any hint of self-consciousness. Even without any real understanding of adult relationships, I knew that it was callous.

The light changed when we pulled into a service station. Union 76. Unabashed patriotism in the middle parts. Instant cool in the shade of the convenience mud hut. The attendants milled around like pill bugs between the Flintstone shanty and the cars docked at the filling stations. Tommy was the first out, duty-bound manhood calling. Lila had to let me out, there were no back doors. Many bathrooms were outhouses then – a side shack overrun with on-the-road laziness and toilet-paper-wad rebellion. The ramshackle head had all manner of scum on the walls and a cheap linoleum floor being reclaimed by the earth. The garbage and its parameters were interpreted loosely. I had gone into the hole alone, which was unusual. When I came out I didn't see Lila or Tommy. I walked along the cement fringe boardwalk of the convenience store, scanning for my mom and her man, and finally caught sight of them off to the side of the parking lot, talking by the car. Lila wasn't really talking, more like refereeing Tommy with himself, her stance cool and easygoing. His expression was like that of a true and loyal right hand of a queen, having to call upon intuition ceaselessly, trying to help and thereby touch the untouchable. I was interested in the dense salty goodness of the brine-candied sausages, and anything Lila was genuinely excited about, so I left them to their mysterious sideshow and went inside.

Lila and I had a pact. It was unspoken but certain. Small as I was, I knew I was her favorite person in the world. The only person she would have been able to talk to had she become unable to speak, had she gone crazy, had her language, her mind left her. She was often specific. She liked to refer to things like Calumet Baking Powder, ask you to hand her the masking tape with "I love you, Mom" written in pencil on it; the blue bowl that looked like it had beaded jewels on the rim; the dish towel Mary had given her eight Christmases ago; the coat Edward hadn't let her buy. Her specificity made her genuine, even when you weren't sure if she was.

Tommy was a garter snake or something as innocuous. I felt he was harmless, but I didn't understand him. He could be fun, silly fun, historical knowledge fun, and you had to respect him for his ability to adapt, to wind his way through the tall grass, though there was nothing obviously useful about him for his sake. Maybe he ate bugs – he had to serve some function in the ecosystem, but he was not built for the tasks he was given in his daily life, and you had to wonder what magic he could have created if he'd been allowed to run free, before he was caught by a badger.

They had met at the university, where Lila had returned after my dad left. I'd stood at the big picture window that was strangely opulent in our little brown house and watched her kick the tires on the blue Volkswagen bug as my dad drove away from the square of cement that said "Edward loves Lila" with my name underneath, all of us inside a big star, as though we were stranded in a supernova together, our names carved for eternity with a large stick. That moment of acknowledged love in 1976 undeniable. The beauty of their characters etched there like leadless pencil tracings. It was all clear and permanent there in the street.

The extreme cold of the air conditioning surprised me and made me feel brave and far from home. I walked over to the cooler with its maddening array of colors and packaging, and picked out an orange juice in a box, like milk. I started down one aisle, eying Nutter Butters, thinking it was strange how they sounded good but were not something I had ever sought out, had only had at a friend's house after school. Noting that this was the aisle with cookies – cookies and crackers were my staples – and knew I must be nearing the Hostess stand. Ding Dongs, Suzy Qs and Donettes. I chose candy depending on my mood, depending on the season, at the 7-11 on the corner by our house. Blow pops and Bubble Yum and ice cream sandwiches. Candy a necessary part of winding down after school, a facet of my grade school personality at a time when most everything was both particular and sincere. I found the place where they shelved canned meat. I had never thought of SPAM, tuna fish, and the prized Vienna Sausages as being in the same category before, but there they were, all in the war rations section.

Lila walked up next to me. She seemed so light, a scarf blowing in the wind.

"Oh good, they have them," she reached in front of me. "Take five or so," she grabbed them off the shelf in an irrational clamor, "They'll be good to have for later."

She left me there to get in line at the checkout terminal, flanked on all sides by magazines, jerky and cigarettes. Tommy came in and went directly to the cooler. I followed Lila out the door.

The rest of the day Lila smoked and told Tommy what it had been like stealing beach chairs with my dad, running down the Eastern corridor to escape/conceive, until they found themselves in Key West. I slept. When I woke in the late afternoon I looked around the car not realizing I was satisfied. Not knowing what satisfaction was. I didn't feel anxious after being so studious. After composing and doing spelling lists at the dining room table, deep-sea diving, whiffle-balling, and running fast. Not having had a moment without duty in all my seven years. I looked out and thought of the hills around us like a rustic dream, what it would be like to be scuffing up their dust, walking between them, to have no distractions but the job of moving and of feeding ourselves. Nothing would come from a can. It would be either pick things or kill, with no forgetting that we had to kill to eat. The nights would be lonely with the ghosts around the campfire, but we would appreciate what we had to do. Appreciate that we were here and able to do it. To have a conscience again, to be born into the killing and the blanket of instinct and the comfort of the dead stars coming to us like needle pricks in my mother's dark curtains.

Coming out of my sleep haze, I felt the pleasantness of being hungry. My mother watched the dark closing in around her. Memories of sitting in the old Chevy smoking cigarettes, her 16-year-old mind tortured by her mother's slow determination to replace her beautiful simplicity with someone else's decadent static dream. I sat up. A plastic bag rustled under my right foot, and I remembered what was in it. The can was compact and sweet-looking with its wrap-around label pictorial of the little wieners in blue and brown, festive as a Southern pig pickin'. I had never popped the lid on a can before and wedged my thumb under the little ring. The pop of the can startled Lila. She turned around and smiled. "Want one?" I said.

"No, that's okay. Well, sure, I'll have one. They started making those when I was a teenager. I'd eat them when I'd go camping by myself on the James River. Those and molasses beans. The water looked muddy there, but when I would dip my cup into it, it was as clear as tap water."

The sausages sat snugly in their compact ring like a carburetor. The tinny meat smell dispersed into the car and filled me with satisfaction. The essentialness of their existence in this vast land, like the motels. The only thing keeping us from falling into the earth.

I pulled them out individually, like fingers. Each an echo of evenings at home, doing calligraphy by the fire. Playing with the dripping wax, molding it into shapes. Making sausage-shaped replicas of my own fingers by pouring wax onto them. Pressing it against my skin like the thin, soft paper of my Grandmother's hand resting on mine in church.

I bit them off, each with the dusky smell of old underwear and the texture of my lips when I covered them in Vaseline. I ate them as we drove past the rolled up boles of hay like corn on the cob sitting in the fields, threshing machines about to be done for the day, horses and cows flicking their tails in the twilight. Shadows appearing from behind a rock and spreading across the vast, cool land, into the wild where the desert rodents ran in and out of its edges.

Dusk on the road. Permanence and a tranquil settling down of mood and heat. Air-packed inside the lime green car. Wind gusting to stir dormant leaves.

Inside, cool and warm. The Nightly News a black and white shrill of movement. It and the movements on the forefront of the horizon a mockery of our stillness.

The sky settled down. Blue cloudiness evaporated into the coming of stars. The extremeness of it was somewhat upsetting. The sun going to the other side of the earth, the earth twisting and turning like a top.

"Honey, we'll be stopping soon. We're almost to Whitefish, where I fished the last time I was in Montana, before you were born. We'll get a river cabin and go fishing in the morning. If you catch anything we can pack it in the cooler and cook it at the next stop, near Elk, tomorrow night."

She and Tommy had been passing a beer back and forth for two hours. It wasn't the same beer, of course, but I didn't keep track. The boxes accumulated in the kitchen next to the back door, then on the back porch. I never saw them clear them out, though they must have sometimes. I didn't know it was trashy to keep stacks of beer boxes, or to give your child Lucky bottle caps that had the puzzles on them. I thought the puzzles were fun – "I see your soapbox racer."

I was always wide wake at night. My bedtime had been set for around ten, but I was routinely allowed to stay up for David Letterman with a glass of cherry shortcake ice cream. Before we pulled into a motel for the night was pleasant, like coming to the end of a race you knew you were going to win. The warm satisfaction of deserving a comfortable bed, and pleasant, meaningful dreams.

The lights flashing behind us were jarring, as

though someone had come upon us in an alley to grab our backpacks and Walkmen. Lila took the beer from Tommy and put it in her lap. She sat up straight, drinking it directly in front of her. Tommy eased onto the soft, rocky earth. The air was still. Crickets sang their evening chirp-poor-whill. I felt the secrecy for the first time. What I had recognized as Lila's self-assurance suddenly became a plea.

Lila opened her door and began to pour out the beer as the officer came over to Tommy's window. I watched as Lila poured out the beer with one hand, keeping the other on her bare leg just below her cutoff jeans shorts. The officer asked Tommy why he'd been going so fast. There was a tension in Tommy's voice that I had never heard. But the calm of my mother's ring-filled fingers pouring out the beer into the sandy earth, the sureness of her steady hand on her leg, made me know it would be fine. Among the blue, red, and white lights flashing against the country darkness, I looked down into my lap at the sausages I held that my mother had gotten me, watching as she tucked the empty beer can into the opening between her seat and the door frame. I held to the thought of eating them as soon as the officer, the traveling salesmen stuck at our threshold, was gone, mimicking my mother's hunted silence.

4

THE MIRAGE
OF MARIO SANCHEZ

When he opened his eyes to the stagnant but tidy room – its high wood walls and floors, the furniture that said, "I know you," but not too much, and the faint light that outside was the hot sun – it told him only that he was there. He had read "The Lost Decade" at the bidding of his wife, but he didn't see the tragedy in it. His wife, Cella, made wood furniture, carving it out in symbiotic patterns that to her went on forever, past the back of the chair and the edge of the cabinet door. He thought her work was nice, and she like an orphan girl radiating through her rags while following the lathe like the back of a centipede, yet he chastised her passion for it and didn't understand the spiritual and philosophical value she saw there. When she'd asked him to leave he'd thought of it simply as an incentive to get out of the house.

Each morning he puts his right forefinger in his mouth, takes it out for a moment, then tastes it. This isn't to check the movement of the air. He feels he has become quite perceptive in his exile, and when he tastes the air he feels as though he's able to taste the distillation of the entire day to come. Today it tastes a little off. Not tragically so, just a little odd - like maybe a mighty, flabby woman will streak past him, or maybe he'll see a toddler trotting along licking a huge pinwheel lollipop the size of its face and suddenly it will trip and fall face down upon it, like a sticky shield that will attract ants immediately. Or some tourist who's had a good day fishing will decide to buy the entire crowd at the Turtle a couple of rounds, which had happened before. It changed the atmosphere of the bar to that of a carnival for an hour or so.

When he'd been with Cella he'd almost always drunk alone, but now every day he came effervescently to the Turtle, called there by what seemed like an obligation to his new identity. There were four bartenders at the Turtle, and he was friendly with them all, but of the four Bob on weekdays and Cat on weekends were his favorites. For the most part he also had more congenial memories of them. Bob let Stephen drink well past his obvious limit on many occasions, which Stephen appreciated. He wasn't exactly a gentleman, but he was a soft drunk; he'd fall off his stool before he'd ever be lewd or obnoxiously belligerent.

It was Wednesday. He'd always hated Wednesdays because he felt that Wednesday was the least dramatic day of the week, save for Tuesday, but he was born on a Tuesday. Wednesdays made him lonely. On Wednesdays he sometimes thought of Cella's flowery air and how she'd always have the windows open and never seemed to be cold. Sometimes on Wednesdays he thought of changing his routine, maybe just taking a walk, but he never had. And lately the Wednesday gloom had been worse; he was running out of money.

"Come on lad," Bob the bartender said in a very fake Irish accent, "Tell me what's got you saggin' or I'll haveta heave-ho ya outa here."

"Nothing."

"But you're sippin' insteada sluggin', lad ..." he patted Stephen's cheeks. "You look sick, sister. Come on, level with me ..."

"Alright, fine." Stephen leaned over the bar, "I'll let you in on the secret, but when I stop comin' in next week some time you gotta cover for me ... say you heard I went snorkeling in the Bahamas."

Bob had his ear cocked right over Stephen's Seven-and-Seven with his eyebrows up.

"I'm broke."

Bob jumped back and slapped the counter, "Get outa here!"

"Down to my last two thousand."

"Now that ain't exactly broke …"

"It's broke to me," he sipped his drink. "Especially here."

"You got that part right anyway … mmm mmm mmm … Mmm! Whatchou gonna do?"

"Don't know ... I may have to call my wife."

"I hear ya, I guess when you retire too early you ain't got no feed when the cows come home," he started wiping the counter and wiped over to another customer, shaking his head as he led himself across the boxing-ring bar. "Mmm mmm mmm."

'Why'd I tell him that?' Stephen asked himself. He felt violated. He hadn't analyzed too many things about himself consciously, but, faced with the potential of poverty, he realized that he felt as though an edge were dulling. He put a five on top of the twenty that already sat on the bar next to his drink and soaked napkin and stood up. It was early afternoon. Bob was resting on one hip talking to his customer with his back to Stephen and didn't notice him walk out of the open-air bar.

Stephen had had four drinks but was still very sober. The sidewalks of the small island were half taken over by elephant-ear sized leaves and as he attempted to stroll he felt self-conscious veering around them, as though people might think he were stumbling. The sidewalk seemed unpaved, uprooted as it had been by Banyan tree roots, uneven, rural-seeming and coarse. What was he going to do without money? The rent for the small furnished apartment with the polished wood floors was a thousand a month.

It was the 27th. He didn't know how long he could last on a thousand dollars – he'd never added up his expenses. Regardless, he'd soon be out of a place to live. He was sweating through his white ramie shirt and envisioned himself suddenly eclipsed by the sun, going mad in a dark alley like Jack the Ripper. 'I was almost a lawyer ...' he thought. But the thought of working felt like the word entrapment. Entrapment. 'Not only trapped, but framed, like a defenseless moron. Framed.' He stumbled through the streets, though to passersby he was only walking; a well-dressed man on his way to meet someone or out on an errand. An ordinarily brilliant soul rotting in the embalmed body of a rich man, flawless. He had walked about three blocks when he turned down an alley-street which had music diffusing into the humid air from someone's back yard. Stephen realized he had a cigarette in his mouth, though he didn't know how long it had been there. He had felt hurried, but deliberately slowed to look through the gaping red hibiscus that seemed to grow wild there to a little white house that was as bright as a bleached white sheet; his wife always used white sheets and shook them out in the breeze of her open windows. There was a clearness around the little house. It had a little wooden blue jay next to the house number. As he passed it he noticed an old gentleman at the side of the house, partially on the lawn, partially on the unpaved drive, which was bordered by an old wooden fence, standing in front of a wooden table.

"Lo there," he waved to Stephen. Stephen stopped

and took the cigarette out of his mouth.

"You lost?" he smiled and looked up from what he was doing.

"No, no," Stephen cleared his throat and lit the cigarette. "Just out for a stroll." He felt his face – he shaved every morning and it was smooth.

"You live aroun' here?" the man had an accent Stephen didn't know. He was pointing bits of color and white onto a board with a small brush.

"Yes, sir."

"You an' your wife?"

"Yes."

"Where's your wife on theese fine day?"

"She's at home – doesn't like the heat."

"Wrong place for her then," he laughed.

"That's what I tell her." He looked past the old man to where things began to get blurry.

"You wan' to come an' see?" he pointed to the piece of wood on the table. Stephen walked among the rough white rocks until he was a few feet from the old man. Their chalk stuck to his black dress shoes. He peered over the space as though the old man were behind a partition, roped off.

"Come closer."

Stephen could see what the old man was painting with his fingers and a brush whose bristles were splayed out like an old toothbrush, like the one he'd had as a kid.

"Ice cream," said the old man. "Not like to-day – real ice cream … glace." There was a man with a cart vending ice cream by white and red bathing cabins on the beach. All the colors were bright and proud, natives. "That man was an entrepreneur," the old man said, "He know where to sell hees ice cream."

"It's wonderful," said Stephen.

"I give eet to you when I finish – tomorrow."

"Oh no …"

"Don' worry, I give to you. I no charge a poor man."

Stephen looked at him. He held his dying cigarette at his side. He looked down at the table and saw everything on it like a pinwheel spinning; brushes, bright circles of paint, tubes, a cloth, the wood with dried and drying paint all over it. "I'll come back tomorrow," he said.

"Good," said the old man. Stephen nodded once. "See you tomorrow," the old man said as Stephen turned and walked as lightly as he could down the rough drive to the sidewalk.

He felt like having a soda, a pop, like when he was a kid. It seemed he hadn't had plain soda since then. There was a store on the corner across the street from his apartment. As he turned onto the sidewalk he glanced back toward the old man who was not there any longer. He looked around and down the alley-street. There were some old men three houses down playing cards at a square table at the edge of a flat driveway. There was an old woman two houses down from them and across rocking on her front porch. There were two chickens criss-crossing each other in a hurry, and the sounds of them and children from a block over. There was the music coming into and out of the air like breath. He looked back up the old man's drive – no old man, no table, no glace. Stephen turned around and went back the way he had come.

Once he was back at the apartment he sat on the bed. 'Man,' he looked around at the contrived living space. 'I'm going to turn into a freakin' nutball.' He lay back and watched the ceiling fan until he fell asleep.

He was hot and crumpled and uncomfortable, wanting incredibly much to let go of his mother's hand, though he knew he couldn't. His mother was beautiful, as all mothers are to their sons.

"Mama, can I please have some glace?"

She looked down at him and out at the sea. He was aware of strings from his brown cut-off trousers tickling his knees. He was barefoot.

"Do you have a nickel, son?"

"No."

As they passed the ice cream cart Stephen noticed it was the old man vending – he being himself as a boy and also outside himself, watching. He looked longingly at the white-handled wooden cart, knowing the sweet smoothness of the mango glace that was inside. The old man took out a shallow paper cone and filled it half with mango and half with mammie ice cream, and handed it to Stephen.

"I'm sorry, sir, not to-day," said Stephen's mother, her red-brown hair blowing almost away from her in the sea breeze.

"Don' worry, ma'am," the old man said, "You get me back an-o-ther day." He bent down to Stephen and whispered as he handed him the glace,

"I no charge a poor man."

Stephen sat up straight in bed with his slicked black hair stuck to his forehead and face. The room was so quiet; he had never known it to be so. The noise of cars, mopeds and people talking, even yelling, seemed to be in a bottle tossed away from the captive and self-contained silence of his room. He sat up in bed, the lining of his light blue pants making a slick sound against his bare legs. His childhood room had been light blue, "sky blue," and his mother had painted white clouds across it. Cirrus and cumulus, he remembered. He put his hands over his face and brought them down slowly, sliding with the thick sweat. He couldn't even feel the ceiling fan it was moving so slowly.

'I know I have a pencil,' he thought, 'If I could only draw something ...' He went over to the table by the window, but there was just a pocketknife on the dark varnished wood. In the kitchen, set off barely from the living room at a depth of four lonely feet, he found a golf pencil in the silverware drawer. It was from Oregon. He smelled it. He sat on the bed with the yellow and white striped sheet that had been furnished him, with his stubby golf pencil and an American Express bill envelope and commenced to draw a portrait of Cella. 'Just a line,' he thought as he tried to define the details of her face in his mind, the real shape of it. 'Just a line to begin – a line is all you need.' He placed the pencil to the envelope and his hand drew a quick, curvaceous line for him; he hadn't realized he was shaking. He quickly retracted his hand from the paper and closed his eyes. 'I'm a bastard ... a real bastard.' He looked around the room; wood table, chairs and nightstand, wood doors, wood-framed clock, driftwood hanging on the audacious stucco wall, wood everything, it seemed; the windows even had wooden shutters. 'It's all drawn,' his thoughts stuttered as he imagined someone, people, making all that his room alone contained. 'Everything.'

He sat still until the dark came and the now strangling complexities of his little room softened; he was a stranger to his room at that hour, yet he felt welcome, as though it had been waiting for him. Soon he would start the throwing up, the convulsive terror of withdrawal, but as the liquid sense of a warm night settled over him he wanted only to sit in peace; a few moments more as captain at the end of his pirated plank.

5

WAX

The smell of chicken in a pan complimented the sound and smell of the fire. Her father was on the couch watching "Wild Kingdom." Lucille had stopped playing the flute in order to listen to her mother in the kitchen, to try and feel what she was doing. She watched a white candle on the light wood dining table flicker a little. It gave to her the illusion of being clear, but she could not see through it. The dining table was shiny, it had come polished when her father bought it from the furniture store where he worked, on sale. Sometimes she worked its surface with a freeze of furniture polish, liking the sound the can made and the feeling of having an unofficial duty to honor her father.

The room was quiet; despite the sound of grease in the kitchen, her mother opening jars and drawers and cabinets, she could hear the low pop of the fire, and the comforting sound of the narrator.

She looked at the cabinet built into the mantle. It was clear glass. Puppets she'd made in fifth grade, pumpkin man and Dracula, sat in front of Anna Karenina and A Tale of Two Cities on the bottom shelf. On the middle shelf were letters that were special to her mother, and Dubliners, A Portrait of the Artist as a Young Man, and Chamber Music, as well as an unframed picture of a painting of a woman standing underneath a tree, holding her child. Lucille had taken one of her mother's books from the shelf one night and read it by the fire. It had felt very strange to take something out of the cabinet. The cabinet gave off the feel of a museum, and her mother had placed the things inside while Lucille had been at school.

She dipped her finger into the pool of wax inside the red candle. It hurt a little, but red didn't hurt as much as white, she remembered. She wondered why they only sat at this table at Thanksgiving. When she was very little, her father used to sit at this table stacking pancakes onto his plate and covering them with syrup, periodically giving pieces to Scuzzy the cat. Now he ate on the couch. Her mother almost always said she'd eat later, and would eat alone in the kitchen while her father was shaving, or after he'd gone to bed. As Lucille lay in bed at night, she felt as though she were spying on her mother.

The wax caps sat on each of her fingers like printers' thumbs; she thought they looked like galoshes. She wanted to show her father, but he was so quiet when he was watching TV before dinner. Really she wanted to ask him to play Scrabble.

She took the wax off her fingertips and melted it together into a ball, which she shaped into a horseshoe. It was for her father, but she didn't know if she would give it to him. She made another ball of wax into a plump heart for her mother.

When they'd lived in New Hampshire, she'd gone sledding with her father often, while her mother stayed inside making bread or sweet potatoes or borscht. "Come on out," her father had yelled, motioning with his hand, when he saw her mother at the window. Her mother would smile at them, then disappear as though she'd been a cloud of steam. She wondered why her mother hadn't let herself enjoy the crisp, pure day when everything is frozen down tight and you walk upon the thin crust of snow as though on a pond.

"Dinner's ready," her mother said, carrying two plates of fried chicken, mashed potatoes and beans. Lucille watched her father as he muted the TV and looked over at her. She thought his eyes looked moist, as though he were about to cry, but he took the plate and smiled up at her mother. "Thank you so much," he said.

"You're welcome. You eating at the table?" she said to Lucille.

"Yes," she said. "I like being near the fire."

"You could sit on the red chair," her mother said,

referring to the rough red patterned chair Lucille had once fallen asleep in that sat on the other side of the fireplace. The next morning her mother had awoken her with a pile of kittens, singing "Rise and shine, baby, Rise and shine, the sun is shining and the day is thine!"

"No, that's okay," she said.

"You going to eat with us?" her father said.

"No, I'm not hungry now."

"Well, I'm sure it's delicious," he said. "You'll enjoy it."

Her mother set the plate in front of Lucille. She smelled like wildflowers. It was a sachet she had made from flowers on the hillside overlooking the drive-in of her hometown. She had come to know the smell as symbolizing memory. The scent was her Great-Grandmother's house on the hillside, her biscuits, the habit of eating in the kitchen. The lilt of her Great-Grandfather playing old mountain songs in the living room, recalling the ways of before he was born.

Her father was still watching "Wheel of Fortune." Vanna White had always fascinated both of them. They had talked about it.

"I like Vanna," she'd said to her father one night.

"She's so consistent, but warm," her father had said.

She agreed with him. She didn't often disagree with her father. He was an agreeable man, she guessed, compared to a lot of people. She wasn't so sure about her mother.

When she'd finished eating, she looked into the cabinet again. A Tale of Two Cities' cover was wildly colorful; it reminded her in an obscure way of a caravan. Once, years before, her father had told her about the desert of Arabia, how it stretched far enough for nomads to spend their entire lives walking through it and not even cross it. They would weave with thread they'd traded spices for; spices that they'd gathered and dried by the fire. They used bright colors, reds, oranges, yellows, like the cover of A Tale of Two Cities. She had asked her father why nomads wandered the desert, and he had said that nomads wandered the desert, climbed mountains, passed through every type of terrain; there were even some in downtown Kansas City.

Did you ever want to be a nomad? She'd asked.

No.

How long do nomads stay in one place?

Not long, usually.

How long?

Long enough to learn what they need to know.

Do they have children?

Sometimes.

I don't want to be a nomad, she'd said.

That's good, her father had said.

Looking over at her father she wondered if he wasn't a nomad, but then she thought he wasn't. Probably in his mind, she thought.

When she finished, she took her plate in to her mother. Her mother was sitting at her little writing table by the stove with a book open which she wasn't looking at. Lucille walked over and put the plate in the big rectangular sink. She felt her mother listening. Her father was listening, too. She saw snow falling outside the window above the sink. She watched some of the flakes blow forth in sudden, hard gusts against the window, while most floated down toward the ground, landing gently, one upon the other.

6

WISH YOU WERE HERE

When I first arrived there was no color. The city looked wet as in a painting and there was a fog but it was not cold. I hadn't been prepared for the feeling of importance around me, or for the idiotic conspicuousness of my big blue backpack. There was the calm of one thing passing and another taking its place without consequence. It seemed the French understood each other. There were the opportunists; hookers and chestnut vendors, the long-armed poets of the café, salon keepers and food dealers opened out into the lush gray air; the students of the Sorbonne with their stung expressions, the heir presumptives and the heir apparents, and there was the river. I didn't talk to anyone for three days except the daytime hotel clerk. To him I'd said good morning because he'd given me a slight smile that seemed genuine. For breakfast I had an apple pastry and coffee and cream from a small grocery that reminded me of the ones in San Francisco, and walked along the quay where they still sold live chickens, and after three days felt very much a part of something important as I had never felt before.

On the third evening Brian arrived at the hotel and on the fourth day the others came. There were twenty of us in the program and we were lucky to have ten men and ten women, they said. It seemed it should have been boys and girls even though we were in college. I met Brian in the baggage room where he was stuffing his beanbag chair of a duffel bag into one of the wire-encased bins while I checked my backpack for a good razor. He had the flushed cheeks of a pure-bred and was the nervous type whose nervousness comes from feeling like he should always be doing something for you. We had coffee and took a short walk together down the streets that were the color of burlap the night I met him, and I found myself much more able to look around when I wasn't alone. He bought me a warm bag of chestnuts which I romanticized very deeply.

We went south to Avignon after five days in Paris. My new school mates played cards on the train; at least one in four of them had thought to bring a deck of cards. They'd all taken up smoking in Paris because it helped them execute their bad French, so it was necessary to open all of the windows in our two compartments. Through the bright, clearer air, past window sails snapping I noticed the stolid green and yellow fields and light blue and white country houses with their calming isolation. The lines of tall, ancient grass swayed like paper waves, and I could feel what it must be like in the fields at night when the owls came out to bless them.

There was the constant noise of the train and the piercing vigor of my classmates; I was glad to go to lunch in the quieter dining car. The people in our group had chosen each other and excluded others with relentless subtlety during the first week of classes. I sat with Rana of Jordan. She had dark brown eyes and only slightly lighter skin, and moved in a delicately erotic way. She asked me which of the guys I liked most, saying she had it in for Paul, who annoyed me by talking louder than everyone else and inserting English when he didn't know the French, which was often. ("Donnez-moi un card. Only un! J'ai un good hand – er – un bon hand!") Feeling pressed, I told her I thought Brian was cute.

That evening we arrived inside the brown walled fortress of Avignon, where I was given the address of a little apartment with a deep, perfectly square bathtub on the fourth floor of a five-story building on the river bed narrow Rue de Felix Gras, from the balcony of which I could just see the top of the Palais des Papes. Classes were held four times a week in a crudely cut, damp stone room two streets over from Felix Gras. Each Wednesday we had an excursion to a place near

Avignon such as Arles, where Van Gogh had lived, or our literature professor's hometown of Fontaine-de-Vaucluse, which had a nice windmill and the feel of the mountains.

By the first weekend it was Rana, Paul, Brian and I having pastisse as though we knew each other at L'Affiche, a jazz club.

"Be careful what you say to him, he doesn't care if you walk out of here with a crooked nose," I told Brian.

"You don't realize what he said about you, do you?"

"I'm not sure you know either."

"Like his drums are supposed to seduce you. Come on, let's get out of here."

"Where?"

"I don't know. He's so cocky."

The drummer of the jazz band looked a lot like Houdini.

I yelled to Rana and Paul as they came stumbling off the dance floor, "Brian wants to get going."

"Where you going, Brian?" Rana said.

"How about the Rio, by the school?"

"Yeah, the Rio's cool! That guy from Australia, the owner, he gave me a free beer just because I wasn't French!" Paul said.

"He's so cocky," Brian said again. I think he was drunker than I was, because I still thought everything was pretty funny.

"Forget about him, how can you be so bugged by some stranger? Is it the fact that he's French? Are you intimidated by French men?" I smiled and put a grape in his mouth. He looked off to the side as he chewed and swallowed with a tightness in his face, and I saw what it'd be like to be with him after the honeymoon was over.

The drummer didn't really look French and alerted my senses like deception does. He didn't look at me like he could have me, but like he was interested in having me. If I'd cut him off with a dirty look he would have looked away quickly and let the drums take over.

"Dancing is so wonderful, and Ass-staire here is such a good dancer," Rana was drunk, but still poised and flirting like a virgin.

I tried smiling at her.

"How you feeling, Marie? Let's go to the bathroom."

Rana put a wet towelette under her shirt and was smiling deep dark red. "So are we having a good time? I just love Paul. It's funny how quiet he gets. He's really sweet. He thinks we should go off by ourselves, but I'm not sure if I want to."

"Well, Brian's pissed off. The drummer came over and said something about how beautiful I was he'd like to eat me or something. I thought French people thought we were bad in bed."

"He's cute, you know. We could get rid of Brian for you."

"I wish I were French and could really talk to him. I'd just walk up, ask him if he'd like to have a drink down the street, and walk out."

"What, is Brian getting on your nerves really?"

"Yeah, why's he act like that ... we barely even know one another."

Neither of us went to the toilet and after we'd

rinsed our hands and run them through our hair, we went back out. Rana had wonderful hair; brown, full and short, and beautiful, full lips. Paul didn't seem to care that the whole rest of the band had been looking at her.

With one final disgusted look at the drummer, Brian did pay the bill, like a true gentleman, and we went out into the late evening. I'd been careful not to step in any dog crap all night because it really was everywhere. The air was so warm that it smelled the way it does in summer at dusk in Oregon. We had all gotten some color in Antibes and I felt healthy. Beer didn't sound good as we walked by the little store that sold yellow custard that came preserved in a small paper container lined with plastic. It was the best thing I had ever eaten and having it right then sounded better than drinking.

Brian was holding my hand as I looked up at the black sky and saw nothing. No moon, no stars. The street was small and rough with pebbles and his shoes made a nice sound against them, like a horse's. "Careful," he was watching the crap for me while I looked up and wondered why they'd come. They had all been to France before and it seemed that they were ceramic and had simply been placed there as salt and pepper shakers on a table and would remain as they were when they came. They still saw French people as romantic excerpts depicted on black and white postcards rushing through the rain with baguettes, holding newspapers over their heads, and never thought that sometimes when they got home they sat on the couch for a long time in the late afternoon when rooms darken without turning any lights on.

Though it had only been a few seconds, I felt like I had been quiet a long time.

"Bougie ... bougie ... bougie!" Rana was saying in a childish voice.

"Stop it!" Brian pushed her further into Paul.

"What's your least favorite French word?" she asked me.

"I wish I knew my heritage better," I said.

Paul stopped dramatically to turn and look at me with his long, clownish face, flat blond hair and pale blue linen shirt. "Random!" He raised his hands in the air and shook them.

"That didn't answer the question, dahling," Rana said as she pulled on Paul and we started walking again.

"I'm gonna get drunk and go to class tomorrow," Paul said.

Brian smiled at me. "Pretend you're French for now."

The Rio was full and a guy who I knew to be a stunt man was drinking a light beer, which I thought was funny. He'd been in there the other two times I'd been in and had told me about how he had worked with Gerard Depardieu. He wore a tight pink faux torn muscle shirt and had long, curly blond hair.

"Hey Joe, one beer and one gin, and what else?" Brian ordered for Rana. Rana always ordered gin.

"Wine wine wine," said Rana.

"And three wines."

"No, silly, Paul will have a straight shot of beer," she said.

"I don't want wine, either," I said. "I'll have vodka."

Rana was acting more drunk than she could have been, so we went upstairs to what was known at our school as the flirting room. We sat on the square cushions in the small carved out area to the left that faced the main room. The room felt very small, even with the mirrors on three walls, and the walls were velvet-colored, with one perfectly square window opened and held at a thirty-degree angle by a hook and chain. It let in the warm air, and caused all the trails of smoke to form twisted designs and pathways that eventually led to the outside world.

"My, this is good. It's really good and I know about gin, you know why? My dad raises it."

"How do you raise gin, Rana?" Paul was acting frattish and putting his hand all over her knee.

"Just like you raise your glass, like this."

"To what?" I asked.

"To our short vacation," Brian said.

"It's like taking a vacance from a vacation," said Paul.

"Only because you don't care about learning French," Brian said.

"Oh yeah, ca va monsieur cool guy, je voudrais un peu de respect s'il vous plait."

"Please, not so formal!" Brian said, smiling.

Paul didn't get it.

"La grammaire de Paul est tres superieuse," Rana said as sincerely as she could.

"Very funny," he said. "Tres blague, tres blague." He raised his glass and drank a lot of what was in it.

The French girls in the room all had long brown hair that fell gentle and straight and shook like tassels, and about half of them were talking to young French men. There were two other Americans in the room, both men, and it was their beards that kept them from getting women. The room was getting packed as three French boys came in and had to stand against the wall.

"Look at that girl over there," said Brian. "She's looking at us like we're not supposed to be here … it's an Australian bar, honey!"

"She's used to acting like that. All French women are bitches."

"Paul! You scary thing," said Rana.

"Everyone knows it."

"Are you drunk?" Brian asked me.

"Are you Australian?"

He just looked at me like he was tired of it.

"Are you drunk?" I was.

"Not really sure," he smiled, "I think it's been too long to tell."

"Just keep drinking then, until you're sure."

"What on earth are you two talking about?" said Rana.

"How tan Brian is."

"Dull." She drew it out. "Would you accompany me to the bathroom, dahling?"

"Not right now, please."

"I really can't hold my liquor."

"I don't have to go."

"Maybe she needs help," said Paul.

"Why don't you go help her, the bathrooms are coed anyway."

"I always forget that!" He had a nice, huge smile.

Rana stood up and sat back down. "That's good gin, I told you."

I whispered to Brian that she'd probably throw up in front of him, possibly even on him. He whispered back that he'd like whatever she did to him.

"You think he likes her that much?" I said after they were gone.

"He'd do anything."

"Well, yeah, to do it."

"What do you mean 'to do it'? What are you, five? No, I think he really likes her."

"Well, that's nice of him." I was getting sick of being with a smart frat boy. "Want another drink?"

"Yeah, what do you want?"

"No, I'll get it." I didn't even give him a chance to get his gentil ass up. The stairs were steep and narrow and I could hear Paul talking and Rana giggling in the bathroom next to the landing. As I was taking the first step down I saw someone turn in at the bottom. It was the drummer. He didn't wait for me to come down and I didn't wait for him either, even though it was obvious that there wasn't enough room for us to pass each other on the stairs. We met in the middle and he said, "Bon soir, such a nice evening, isn't it?"

"Oui, c'est encore chaud." His skin was coarse looking, like freshly rolled wheat dough. He was smiling and I looked at him and he looked at my mouth. I kept it frozen in this pose that I thought might be nice to look at, but eventually bit my bottom lip and asked him what he wanted to do. I said:

"Comment est-ce que tu desires faire ca?" which is the most elementary way of saying, 'How do you want to do this?'

"Comme ca." He took my hand and we went down the stairs and right through the corridor of the bar and out the door. It was a lot warmer than I'd wanted to admit to myself, because warmth makes me feel good, but lonely sometimes. Sometimes being there was so overwhelming that I didn't want to upset it and the warmth made it worse. I wished we were in Paris because small towns even in France can feel trashy but not in that seedy glamourous way. In the country it's more like a carnival. The purity is sacrificed to showmanship and the clean air makes the morning all the more painful in its lonely wasted loveliness.

"Tu es jolie, mais Americaine …"

Mais Americaine; I laughed. He took it for granted that I understood things. "Oui, je suis un tramp Americain."

"Qu'est-ce que c'est qu'un 'tramp'?"

"Whore."

"Oh, non." He stopped to look at me, then kissed me. It was very nice. He had straight brown hair that fell around his eyes like a show curtain.

"Est-ce que tu veux voyager a Paris?" I said.

"Oui, jolie fille." He was speaking slowly. "Quand est-ce que tu veux y aller?"

"Maintenant."

"Ca va. Tu es folle?" He asked me if I were crazy.

"Oui."

"C'est bien ca. C'est un bon idee d'etre fou."

"Oui oui."

"Oui," he looked right at me again. He cared nothing about my friends. He was trying not to smile to hide any eagerness he must have felt.

He laughed as we walked by a brightly lit bar whose light and free feeling lit the sidewalk and crowd of singers in front of it. Their clamor was so elegant it sounded almost like a siren as they swayed together. But soon we'd be in the Montmartre, where the drunk outnumber the sober twenty to one and the theme of the neighborhood is dripping and scheming and saying you're sorry when you want to go home.

The train was not full, and it felt more empty than it was, especially in the club car. Around two a.m. as it was pulling slowly over the barrier between the countryside and the city I began to think. It is always a mistake to think while you're coming out of drunkenness. We'd had a few drinks on the way to the station, and on the train we'd had several more until I felt I might pass out. I knew I could get really drunk again in Paris and had excused myself from the café to go sit in a compartment nearby with a man from North Africa who gave me a piece of sticky fruit which he cut up with a knife from which he took pieces. I hadn't drunk steadily enough and it gave the eventual seemingly lucid illusion of having drunk nothing at all. Houdini was strong and could hurt me, I thought, though he seemed alright and comfortable to be around, but I was also no longer attracted to him. He'd been a drummer all his life, wasn't educated but read a lot, and was thirty-eight. If I did sleep with him I would have to be careful. I knew him now. There was nothing in it for me anymore. I thought of how I would have felt in the middle of the night and remembered when I used to be able to pass out and wake up clean. Now I hardly ever slept through the night and in the morning I knew I hadn't slept but had only come to. I would have left him in the bed of a ragged hotel on an obsolete floor at five thirty when everything everywhere is gray, even in America, and the only romantic part about it would have been how I had left him and walked through Paris just before it began to get light and gotten my ticket and gone to get an apple pastry just as it was getting light, and ridden the train back alone with the clammy hot feeling of too much so never enough until I was back in bed at my little apartment on Rue de Felix Gras with secrets to tell and a pissed off Brian who was no less of a fine guy for being such a jerk. I thought it was all better than going to bed early but it was a long trip and I was very tired.

I went to the back of the train and watched for the station. The lights came up confidently and clearly as those of an official place, but with the promise too of relief, like reaching home after a walk in the snow. I jumped off as Houdini was eating his last few pieces of ice. He lived near Paris anyway. His friends would bring his drums. I knew he'd wait for me a long time so I went and bought a ticket for the five o'clock to

Avignon and walked out of the station.

It is very pleasant in Paris always because even when it has been raining and raining and raining you know that the rain has done something. To the city and to the people there. It was a fine mist of rain that night as I crossed one of the many small and beautiful bridges to an odd creperie and sat and watched the old man in the back drinking his café and reading a book after he had made me something to eat, and I drank coffee and ate the spinach crepe and wondered why he stayed open all night. I've heard that old people don't need as much sleep and I wondered if he missed it. His wife was probably gone and he was enjoying something like I was watching him, only he had learned to do it alone.

I sat drinking the café he had taken from the large bronze espresso machine and turned away from the old man reading to see, in a moment, a couple walking by looking very picturesque in their dark green raincoats. If they had looked in they would have seen a young woman at a small square table alone surrounded by other empty tables and the paintings on the walls. If either of them were very observant and had glanced far back enough they would have seen the counter drawn straight across and the large bronze espresso machine, but would doubtless have missed the blurry old man sitting just beyond it reading with a little white cup etched around his forefinger. They didn't look up, though, because they were together and arm in arm and very happy for the immediacy the rain brought to their relationship. I thought they were probably going home to make love and was jealous but I had the old man and he had had what they had but now he hadn't and was an old man and was I an old man – no, I wasn't, not like him because I hadn't had it yet and the thought made me apprehensive and I knew then that he missed it and that that was why he stayed open all night. I knew also that I was probably all wrong and that all the couple had was a walk in the rain and that he was just an old man who hated his wife and that I had drunk much too much and was, first and foremost, a student in a foreign country.

7

100 YEARS FROM NOW

I have only ever heard my mother call one man "Sir." I call him Capt. Edie, and the only person who calls him by his first name is his wife. He is a doctor. But mostly he is one who never stands on ceremony. Ten years ago he told my mother she had to quit drinking before it killed her. They sat at his kitchen table and he looked across and told her, "No more beer." My mother is a writer.

Out back of his house now he cooks two steaks, one medium, one rare. The flames sear through the meat, turning its blood brown. I think it smells good even though I won't eat it. Mrs. Edie has been vegetarian for 25 years.

"Did you graduate yet?" he asks me.

"Magna Cum Laude."

"Good. Good ... Your health good?"

"Yes, Captain. Except I finally got the chicken pox last year. That was bad. They had to give me pills to stop them coming."

"I had a surgery last year. The doctor asked me when I'd had my coronary bypass. I never had one. I had a coronary without knowing it. My blood pressure's good now. I hope to get ten years more out of life ... I know that's nothing to you."

I looked at him, not wanting to disagree. "Ten years is a long time."

"I have to get this perfect for her." He turns the steaks another time and when he takes his off the flames go all the way down.

Their house has many things in it. Collections from when Mrs. Edie shut her gallery down and things brought home from Japan and Europe. Many things make squares; tables, paintings, sets of things. Capt. Edie has a collection of 25 muskets from more than one war. They are made of metal and wood designed as simple as death. They hang on the wall safely, in a hallway filled with painting supplies. In his bedroom is a cabinet full of scrim-shawed whaling tools made of ivory.

Mrs. Edie brings vegetables and bread to the table as we sit. Capt. Edie holds a curiously large pepper mill above his meat. He pushes the top and we look over, responding to a sound like a battery-operated battle toy.

"What the expletive is that?"

"It's a pepper mill."

"It lights up."

"It was a gift."

"It's heavy."

"They're fancy people, the Morrisons."

"Must be the batteries."

"You have another book coming out?" Capt. Edie says to my mother.

"It's due in six months and she only has eighty pages!" I'm trying to be light, or carefree. It's just something I throw out there. A light gibe, maybe. I never teased my mom about anything.

"Miss, in a hundred years it's not going to matter if she starts today, next month or next year!"

But it would if she'd never started the book or never finishes it, I think.

"How is your steak?"

"Terrific."

"If it's too rare we can put it back on, the coals will be hot almost an hour."

"It's great, Sir."

"You should never sign a contract until you've finished, then you know it's yours," he says.

When I was eight, Capt. Edie gave me a scrimshawed ivory bodkin made into a necklace with four-pound test.

Tonight I lie on their couch under heavy blankets to fend off the severe air conditioning wondering what it will be like a hundred years from now and which things will matter and which won't. It seems someone will keep the scrimshaw and the muskets, as they are already so old.

8

THE ROOT CELLAR

Maren had observed him like a ghost. She knew he still allowed himself to listen to John Coltrane and drink scotch after work and into the evening, even though he'd told himself he wouldn't and would ride his bike after work instead. At least it kept him from thinking about her too much. His fear of alcohol dependence was a small price to pay. He had gotten the apartment while he was studying for the bar. She had nodded to herself when she saw it; it was much like the one he'd had his first year of law school; white, sterile, uncomplicated by history. Within his comfort zone. He set up the calfskin chair and ottoman his grandfather had given him next to the wall of windows. He termed this his "command center," after his father's home office. His father was a tall, facetious assistant vice president of customer relations, always a little too fat and self-satisfied to make it all the way up. Marc bragged that his father had once been considered a potential nominee for California governor, knowing deep down that it had been a shot in the dark, something an assistant chief of staff had thrown out at a cocktail party and no one had taken seriously, except in a fraternity frame of mind. "Yeah, Bud, go for it! I can see that face on yard signs ... you're better looking than the governator!"

His father had had a heart attack four months earlier. His grandfather had died of a heart attack at 61 and he knew it wouldn't be a long time for his father. His mother had herself and his father on Weight Watchers and tried her best with her limited knowledge of what was healthy to keep him fit. But he snuck cheap beer onto their sailboat every other weekend, skiffing around the bay by himself. He was a man of almost no real ambition, but with enough respect for pampering to keep up the appearance of having some in order to get paid. Marc had never stood up to his father, or even refused a can of Bud from the doughy hand of the man he had lied to since he could talk. He remembered his father asking him about his dreams when he was little, because he was on ADD medication and nightmares were a side effect, and he'd told him he had dreams of sailing when he had actually dreamed of snakes piling on top of him, slithering around his room and into his orifices.

Marc came out of the shower, the start of a Saturday with no agenda except to review some documents for Monday, which could wait until Sunday. He liked waiting until the last minute sometimes, just to be rebellious. He sat in front of a chocolate croissant and coffee. He looked down at them sitting on the bamboo mat, then out the window across the room. From that angle all he could see was the building across the street, but from the command center chair, he could see the river. It was finally the beginning of summer, but this didn't matter to him much. He would go hiking by himself, or bicycling with Real from work, a skinny fifty-two year old with nothing to offer in the way of conversation except Wall Street Journal article summaries and recaps of the two trials he'd had that year.

He looked at his bookshelf. On the bottom was Maren's copy of Tender is the Night. He hadn't been able to get rid of it and realized that he always thought of how it was there, trying to hide on the bottom shelf, but never acknowledged it. He thought about watching Five Easy Pieces and making out on the couch with her the summer before, so thin and beautiful her little body in his big lap, and making love with her in the warm night in the little house they'd shared in law school that was like a farm house and suddenly wanted a cigarette. He had one in a plastic bag that he'd saved from law school, his emergency cigarette for exams that he had never smoked because he had her to call instead.

He remembered the night of the Christmas party, afterward sleeping alone in the room with no curtains, curled up waiting for someone to tell him what to do.

"Oh my goodness!" she had said, smiling and starting to traipse across the back lawn of his new boss' house in Beaverton, the lawn dewing over in the late night cold. "That was the dullest thing ever ... an insult to the word party!"

She'd looked over at his face, stern as she stopped in front of her car door, her expression falling into disappointment like a child being reproached after thinking they'd done well in the Christmas play.

They had gotten in the car as at dawn when everyone doesn't talk out of respect for others' sleepiness. Onto the cold suburb road they had driven, it reminding her of long drives she would take alone in college, watching the silhouettes of the hills around Corvallis fold out onto each other, knowing she wasn't alone. She had grown up outside of Sullivan, New Hampshire, on 20 acres. She had told him about the deep yellow Banny eggs that were almost all yolk and the wild turkeys running out of the forest and hanging out with the chickens in the sometimes dusty, sometimes muddy clearing between the chicken house and the pond. What she missed most, she had said, were the cool evening frog songs that would come up from the bordering forest that hid a little bog about the same time as the fireflies started blinking on and off like little lit up potato bugs while she and her brother hit the last few volleys across the badminton net. This hadn't struck a chord with him until he hung out with her the summer of their third year of law school when they lit candles in the back yard of their little farm house and he had felt the summer evenings come on strong like they had never existed before.

After the "party" he had floated through a red light without realizing it, and turned into a strip mall. The grocery store was still open. He parked as far away as possible from it, so far away that she wondered where he was going when he got out of the car. She sat watching him walk, he always looked heavy when he walked, being so tall and thick and dressed in clothes that didn't fit him.

She got out and walked after him at the pace he was going, watching him enter through the automatic doors as though through a portal. He wandered down a fruit and vegetable corridor and over to the side aisle, stopping in front of the pomegranate juice to stare at it. She came to stand beside him in line.

"Is there anything else we need?" he asked.

She thought of several things. "No, I don't think so."

In the car his body felt heavy as though he had gone swimming in his clothes, and he did not turn the key.

"What's wrong?" she had said, knowing how futile the question was.

"I'm not like those people, they weren't even talking to each other. Where were they? Did you see the flowers, silk roses! in the bathroom?"

She was relieved, until she realized she couldn't respond honestly without pissing him off, because she knew he'd take the job anyway.

"You don't have to talk to them, they don't have to

be your friends," she said, even though she couldn't imagine working every day with people who had spent three years studying to end up defending insurance companies and seeming fine with it, and for whom alcohol didn't even make them interesting.

She thought of the young man, pre-law school Marc he had told her about. He who had gone after work to have a drink at Smyth's around the corner from his tiny apartment in Manhattan, then sat on the roof reading J. M. Coetzee (which she knew was a problem, but blamed it on immaturity, his lack of experience), watching the neighbors barbecue and feeling a foreigner. This was the man she wanted to love, not the check shirt insurance pinch-hitter sitting next to her in the Volvo. But then again he had also been a paralegal in Manhattan, and before that had worked for Wendell Wilke in D.C. He had been turning his clock key in the wrong direction maybe always. And his parents, a mother who kept his room exactly the same, down to the little twin bed not made for bringing anyone home, and the model sailboat and the blue walls, and his father, the might as well be an insurance adjuster or shoe salesman who had a speaker in his pillow piping classical music to help him sleep.

"Let's go," she'd said.

He looked at his Blackberry. Her number was still in there. He felt a wave of happiness as he thought of hearing her voice. He looked out the window at the Steel Bridge, black and harshly industrial, reminding him of nothing but black-faced coal miners he'd seen on the cover of a book at Powell's earlier that week, no relation to the Steel Bridge, only just as professionally removed from him as those who'd built it. After a while reading Coetzee in the command center, he wound his way around the Columbia to a trail he'd found in a book and hiked until he almost passed out, stopping to sit on a log eating red beans from a can and wanting to cry but not allowing himself to, fearing this would be the beginning of the end and he would end up moving to Hood River and opening a motel.

After work on Monday he felt a little satisfaction at turning in a brief he'd been working on since the week before. He walked two blocks over from the big pink reflecting pool of a building where he worked to Mary's Club and sat in the corner drinking scotch and thinking of her body in the flashing light of the credits of Venus, and her smiling in the tall grass on the top of Mt. Pisgah. They had hiked the gentle hill that was a mountain in Eugene together at least once a week after classes, taking the thin trails through the grass, sometimes sitting in it, he in his big straw hat. He had told her of his grandfather who was fond of wandering, sometimes walking into the forest on family trips in the valley, not to return for hours. He watched the young blond woman in front of him dancing topless for twenty minutes, then went home and sat by the window in his white apartment with the big black bird Picasso and the Diebenkorn he didn't even like until it was time to masturbate and fall asleep counting backward from a thousand, just to be sure.

In the morning he felt like he had melted into the bed and couldn't move. It was cold on the verge of raining outside his white down comforter, the window was open. It was grey inside and out. He decided to take a personal day and called his assistant.

He thought of her right after he got off the phone. They'd gone to Bend to wade in the river and he'd asked her if she wanted to live there after law school. He had always said things, just to see what they felt like. He didn't really mean them, but she took them to heart. She wanted to live in Bend, have a big garden and a root cellar, can jam and sell it at the Christmas market. "Real life isn't like law school," he'd said. "But that's the cool thing about Portland, we can have those things there, too. I can't start my career in Bend." She'd gotten a job at the courthouse as a clerk while he studied for the bar.

They'd gotten an apartment together initially, until she got tired of feeling herself become obsolete.

He put on some running shorts and his grey Princeton t-shirt and walked over to the courthouse. He sat on one of the benches next to the elk fountain, across from a man with a miner's beard who was smoking with ruddy yellowish fingers swaying. He felt this man knew something. He felt that this man, more than any other, could give him advice. He looked up to see Maren walking up Madison Street toward the courthouse. He watched her, a field mouse, walk across Fourth Avenue. He ran across the park and caught up to her.

"Marc." She looked horrified, but she was not surprised.

"Hi!" he smiled big and intensely as he had not done since his father had given him a stuffed elephant for passing preschool.

"Hi."

"How are you?"

"I'm okay."

"Good. Listen, come have coffee with me."

"We have a hearing at 8:30."

"I want to move to Bend."

"Good for you."

"Bend ..." he waited for it to sink in. "Let's move to Bend."

"What?" she smiled like someone had just fed her silicone pudding.

"I want to move to Bend with you."

"I'm seeing someone," she lied.

"Who is he? Is he a lawyer? Do I know him?"

"He makes bikes."

"Nice. He makes bikes."

"It's none of your business."

He looked at her. His eyes looked like they were made of buttons.

"Law school was a mistake for me. I hate working here. I thought you wanted to be a big corporate lawyer, your dream of living in the West Hills ... I thought you had to live in a city," she said.

He looked at her. She was so pretty, she had her mother's Native American cheekbones.

"I don't care about that as much anymore."

"You wouldn't be happy without your career. Even though I never understood how doing insurance defense would help you become a corporate lawyer. There aren't any corporate lawyers in Portland, and if there are, they're all very, very old." She missed him for a second. She remembered sitting in the park across from him by their house in law school where they would meet during lunch or after classes. His face had reminded her of a pencil tracing, delicate, like Rimbaud's. He had been so willing to lean back into the grass and just sit there. He had said, "I like being quiet with you."

He felt old. He felt very, very old. He couldn't walk away, but he did. He kissed her on the cheek in his mind and walked down the sidewalk back over to the strip of mostly empty benches. He glanced at the miner, still smoking and swaying into the distance. "I don't need a root cellar," he said under his breath as he passed the older dark-suited attorneys and their youthful colleagues in bright unmatching shirts and ties, on their way to morning call. He wandered toward Pioneer Square, feeling comforted by the ornate buildings he knew had been designed by A.E. Doyle, comforted by the Williams & Sonoma bowls he recognized from his mother's kitchen in their display window. He thought of Christmas with his family socked in at the beach near the artichoke fields, little trips, packages of bliss that pockmarked his now unchecked flat-lining trajectory.

Rimbaud had been a sailor; he had sailed to Africa to trade slaves. Maren had never been able to reconcile the boy who had written the most beautiful poetry she had ever read with the man who participated in the taking of the most beautiful thing that existed.

9

PIT STOP HUSBAND

Bonner and West still had seven hours to go before they got to Seattle – a little further in Montana, the panhandle of Idaho, then into Washington, the entrance into which always made Bonner sentimental. West, her husband, had been messing with the sounds on his tiny "pocket" noise synthesizer that he'd gotten in Bozeman.

They were in Western Montana and were about to pull over for a dinner stop, which would break things up a bit. Bonner hoped West would leave the tiny noise machine in his seat. They had been married for seven months and he hadn't finished reading the only book he'd taken up – Catch-22 – but he'd sit and fuss with the noisemaker for hours. He was a musician and a painter, not a writer; she understood that. But she was starting to fear that he was damaged or limited in some irreparable way she couldn't understand.

The bus parked in a lonely and hidden corner of the parking lot, in danger, it seemed, of being overtaken by the ditch of brambles growing next to the road. She couldn't imagine the circumstances for being there ever being "vacation" or "relaxation," though she could imagine a father, amped up on speed traveling with his family, on the run from one situation to another, billing it as such. There was a black hole marked with white lines all around the place, so you'd never be disturbing anybody.

As they filed off the bus in the dark early evening of the first Fall chill, a group of smokers gathered on the concrete walkway in front of the motel. West took his time getting off, still fiddling with his electronic noise machine. Bonner thought of how there are a fixed number of notes, but an infinite number of sounds, and how this was no less true of the sounds coming from his plastic box, though they were of the distorted variety. The smokers quickly took up space around the fluorescent lighting, feeling the immediate bond of addicts.

Bonner scanned the crowd for hot girls – there was one, wearing short, short cutoffs and a glittery green tanktop with a heart whose iron-on material was flaking off. The young woman's skin was smooth and brown, her hair dishwater blond. She wore flip-flops. Her teeth, or something about the severity of her face, betrayed her rough existence. She seemed to be with a boy, more rough-hewn than she was, someone who, she guessed, could not get through the night without "getting into some shit," or planning the next time when he might likely do so. They were sharing a cigarette and talking loudly, engaging the rest of the crowd.

"Aren't you hungry? Don't you want food?" Bonner thought. "Shut up."

West walked slumped over like someone traversing a riverbed through a rainstorm, heavy with rocks. *Clomp, clomp.* His shoes were too big, part of the lot left by his dad, which also included a closet full of too-large suits that no one knew what to do with. Bonner walked behind him toward the Shari's. From behind, his figure resembled a burlap-sack. Yes, she thought, as she watched him walk heavily through the concrete parking lot – I'd gotten away with it, that is what I thought. Yes. For the love of ... keep walking. Walk until the cement turns to grass and steppe and sand, walk to the edge of the water, walk under water, till you get to the ice, keep walking until you turn chemical, for a brief time digital, then analog again, until you turn into musical notes, into blips on the screen in Pong, into the wind careening through the near-winter trees, into that which makes up one frog, and then another ... hop, hop ... hop, walk until you turn into motes blown off the dust of that shelf. I'm behind you, she whispered, and felt him hear her ...

Shari's, imposing in stature, in reputation, like the one base camp in all of Newfoundland, stood in front of West, the wandering soldier. At the edge of what felt like the perimeter, the edge of its property line, he turned around. "I feel like a big, juicy steak. What do you feel like, honey?" He was looking over his shoulder, half-ragged, determined to get there. Still carrying his martian communication device.

He should have been born in the '70s, she thought. It would have made more sense. West looked pretty homeless, young homeless; the homeless who is assumed to still have a choice. Bonner pictured shit stains, hard to decipher on his brown, corduroy pants; she had definitely heard homeless things come from his mouth, seen him hiding under the cheap Formica dining table & staring at her with wild animal eyes while she lay in bed reading fifteen feet away, dry Georgia leaves in refugee piles against the line of windows behind him; Fall creeping in on his psyche, reminding her of the threat of being stuck indoors with him, late nights painting upstairs in the art studio/school where everything was child-sized while she drank wine on the kitchen floor with Adrian Orange, swapping stories of exes, assuming one day West, in all his manic glory, would be another.

Like witnessing an intense storm, Bonner had watched West pace in a speedy circle after not smoking weed all day, an experiment, like sleep-deprivation – using one's mind like a drug. This and other things were made innocuous at crucial times by his trust fund – to everyone except she who must sleep next to him, afraid-awake with intimate knowledge, always a little bristled and wondering when the fiend would rise, encore.

At times it was as though West were made of dead fingernails, a human but unfeeling sculpture of parts unwanted – and the fact that no one but Bonner could see it, though she could tell that others sometimes felt it like a premonition, caused the feeling of a howling wind relentlessly blowing through their lives.

It was cold. Not the dead, hard cold of the world being frozen down tight like a block of ice, nor like snowflakes falling and sticking on gloves in the aftermath silence of January in Peterborough, New Hampshire in thigh-high snow wearing mother's borrowed, fleecy boots and going out for air; nor the grainy, trapping, forgotten cold of a dead bird found in a tiny berm while sledding, nor of the birdsongs of early twilight that stung like blown glass shattering peacefully across the field between the old farmhouse and the edge of the woods, but an early cold, an eternal, blowing cold, a foreshadowing presence of ice on the skin.

She watched Shari's reclaim West through her sturdy metal door. She was next, but didn't want to go. Back into all that unclearly-remembered time before birth, what is called the universe. She was in the middle of everything after, the pain of death relived, a foundling on a short night walk against one wall of a heavily-breathing sea. A dead horse ridden in the familiarity of a lonely marsh filled with stone-streams in the pre-lighted dawn of an impending, threatening day.

West's paddle feet inside the too-big, plastic "Earth shoes" he'd inherited from his father and wore so heavily disappeared inside, and Bonner suddenly remembered what it felt to walk through a parking lot alone. There was a sudden whiff of spring and her nose perked, like a spaniel's.

Inside, the cafe was warm and busy. There was a man alone at one of the tiny booths for two, drinking coffee and smoking. Apparently they still let people smoke inside restaurants in Montana. A few dusty-looking men sat at the counter, and there were voices from behind other booths. West always got excited about ordering dinner for his wife – he liked the feeling of providing, his new favorite thing how easy it was to choose and order things for her. He liked the immediate feeling of accomplishment it gave him.

Bonner stood in the parking lot, washing herself in the absence of stars caused by black asphalt reflected in the sky. After a time, she turned to study the highway's lonely, man-made horizon – a road they'd been following out of what they had accepted as their shared necessity, taking turns down one path, then another. This one a gash through haunted Western woods to visit Bonner's frail mother, whom West had never met, and Bonner had not seen for many years.

What Bonner saw on the dark, brimming horizon was a hideous joke, something she hadn't noticed on their sleepy drive in; something that must have passed by them like a trolling shark on the other side of the bus. An old, falling-apart motel. It reminded her of the ones she and her parents had stayed in on trips when her mother still pretended that there were things like fishing and camping and driving. It was an open cross-section of death, failure, execution.

The walls were missing, each room displayed placidly as a diorama of the carcass of ghosts. In it, beyond death. The motion of what people are when they seep into the ground inside their own graves – the six feet under of misspent hours, of rest and of restless waiting; the receding vessel of escape and indecision – a cross-section of one of the rotting, reclaimed strata of every creature's – our – time here. Trading places; deadly-weighted time. Remnants of dropped toothpaste and cum puddled on top of never-washed comforters put in a pile just before dawn, just before the last day of operations.

The colors were missing, faded to the point of creating a new color that could only be seen in the reflection of a near-blinding light of the motel's last setting sun. The people from the bus smoking, many of whom had filtered into the Tom Thumb and Shari's, had once smoked outside that motel, talked about the hunting and fishing in the area, the things they had killed, and their children. They had smoked cigarettes restlessly, crushing them out on the asphalt.

Inside Shari's, West stood beside a large man in a baseball cap, made modest by strokes of grease that crept down his forehead like a crown. The man asked where West was from. He said Georgia. He said he was ordering dinner for himself and his wife, and that they were traveling to Seattle to see her mother, whom he had never met. Proud tale.

The waitress came; 51 and clearly a smoker. Her status given away by the somehow archetypal wrinkles around her mouth. West ordered one steak dinner, rare, and one steak dinner, medium-well. Bonner came in and stood beside him. She looked especially clean in her milkweed-blue dress. Her cleavage was on display, and she liked that just then. When the waitress leaned over to take West's money, Bonner ordered a piece of blackberry pie. In college she had enjoyed walking from the tiny Chinese slumlord house she rented by the river that had mushrooms growing through the carpet in the closet about half a mile to the nearest Shari's to buy a whole sugar-free blackberry pie: $5.99. When she ordered this shard of memory, West looked at her like she had betrayed him.

They walked close, puffy-vest flanking and nearly touching dirty white, too-large Wile E. Coyote T-shirt, back across the mineral black parking lot to the stock of game pigeons pecking under the incubator security lamp, buzzing with similar summer insects. Bonner honed in on her right away, the tan, scared one with the green spaghetti straps. Only perverted men went down on the first date, and only sleazy cunt girls who blew men in the back seats of Greyhound buses wore spaghetti straps.

In the darkening bus, Bonner could smell the steak on West's breath and hear the faint sound of his alien noise machine coming from his headphones. She turned toward the evidence of outside's existence that would soon be streaming by like a large comet. Bunny in the moment before the hawk comes down. Night's end after drinking: can't ... imagine ... taking ... one. more. step. Only right then she really couldn't. She had stopped walking. The only consolation before having been that no one was beside her, that at least she had spared them the aftermath.

They were given the ten-minute warning, and she got off the bus. West, still looking down at the buttons of his noise-machine, touched her butt as it went by.

"Where you going, sweetie?"

"To get the last of the evening's air."

The girl with spaghetti straps was smoking another cigarette. Her boyfriend, attached to her by a secure tether, ate a cheeseburger, dropping ketchup on the ground.

"Where you guys from?" Bonner asked.

"Spokane."

"Tulsa."

"We just met."

"Oh, really?"

"We're in love, though."

"That's amazing."

"Yeah. Soul mates."

"So, you guys know a good place to get some weed in Spokane? I think we have a long layover there, and my husband needs some. He gets a little crazy without it."

The girl looked down at her cowboy boyfriend's tight jeans hugging their boots. He looked at the ground and stuffed the last of his cheeseburger in his mouth, ketchup slothing onto the side of his lip.

"I know where I can get you some," the girl said.

"Great. If you wouldn't mind, speak to my husband when you get back on the bus. The blond one with the noise machine."

With that, Bonner walked toward a ranch-style cement building across about a hundred white painted parking spaces that read: Polebridge, Montana in scaffolding letters. It was empty, but the lobby door, an entrance to a bell-diving metal pod, was open. It was to Bonner like walking into a meadow as the breeze of the closing door blew by. The tree down the street, seen from a reclined position in the yard, seemed so tall, promising. In the middle of the fluorescent lobby, surrounded by tiny numbered boxes made for a paranoid, wayward, or practical few, she imagined getting a letter posted there.

Outside, the bus started up. Bonner watched it with excited skepticism as it moved slowly away, West still inside. She did not imagine that he was distracted, really, but that he'd had a delayed reaction to the motion, having been filled with the noise of her noiseless, taraxacum blowball encounters with the world.

10

THE SMALLEST OF ENTRYWAYS

She had her head cocked like a winter bud. The green faded tile floor with flecks of red, green, yellow color squares is much lower and me sliding around on it like drips of condensation down her window glass. The pots and pans, in and out of the cupboard, Lila's Brussels sprout seeds sprouting on the windowsill with the quiet light breaking in in the morning before we wake up and staying there until I go into the puce living room to cut paper. Lila why are you so rough with the delicate antique flower thin China like a W. Whitman hillside? You take them from their stacks or do some such while I take the pans out and look at the metal vent, sliding on the big pot, the one for black-eyed peas and spaghetti. You don't want me in there, but you do. You want me to see. To see you make bread, to see you mix the yeast in the flour, to see your effort. Edward doesn't care. He won't even give you money for a coat, but he buys coffee. He's better than you, he thinks, because he didn't have me. You had me to see. At least you gave me the kitchen. A whole shelf above the stove. Spices. You are an artist, Mama.

Black marks floating notes very much more than I could ever ask for when I'm alone. Thank you for giving me the option to diffuse into my room and into yours like the smell of a growing leaf. You sit outside my room, on the couch but that isn't that far from my room and you listen. I didn't notice because of how happy I am. You go into the kitchen and you start typing. You shouldn't be typing while I'm on the flute. It's disruptive and you only type when I'm home. I think you don't do much of anything when we're not home. I think you watch "Guiding Light." I know you watch it because I've watched it with you when I had the flu. You know what's going on, I can tell.

The only thing at all like the kitchen is the garden. There are the stairs that then were good and the white trellis, all of these things donated you could say by the old pair who lived here before us. Squatting and dropping seeds – plip, plop, plip – into the divots in the rows like cake batter, little beans and tiny melons dna-ed and happy to begin. The fence was nice back then and the honeysuckle bush I would run to like a comet.

At the Lincoln Log school the kids said push it push

the snow in huge plow like fashion with their tiny red and white mittens over by the cannons at the park, and even then I stayed behind with the teacher because it was warm and I didn't have to do anything. Taking off their wet things slick with melted snow bragging like Montessori kids. Picking my nose in the song circle. Nobody noticed until the teacher said, stop that it's not clean. There are piles of garbage on my bed. I can only use one cup or I get yelled at: "Use the same cup!" There are moth larvae crawling on my ceiling. I listen to Van Morrison and Peter Tosh before bed to drown out the typing and yelling. A Cricket in Times Square and later a cigarette in the dark and a Hershey's Chocolate tin with a nice old-fashioned girl as an ashtray.

The table is very big and the circle is easy to cut. At the next station there are fractions. Emily, my friend with the bowl cut, tried to swallow her tongue and now her mouth sounds full when she talks. She turned her back and I colored Nebraska yellow and she got very upset. I helped my friend/crush Alexander tie his shoe. They only let me skip one grade because we came back from the island. It wouldn't have mattered if I'd graduated then. The horseshoe crabs taught me everything.

Edward wasn't there and then he was there hiking and playing baseball and telling me that my socks smelled like cat pee before we went to Herfy Burger with the cow head plastic bust over the entrance like he and Lila and I used to. Lila and Mary and Michael and I shopped at Prairie Market.

This was before Winchell's was there even and before the first store I went to with bar codes lost their last cash register with any sense of itself. Gum was the first to go, then canned stuff and later cooler items and even finally bulk foods. Nothing was dusty anymore. Edward became the bottom of some old brown stairs trapped near the university, tiny cakes on my plastic blue and white doll plates.

The July of my seventh year I tried to become part of the blackberry bushes that flanked the old garage we had never once used for anything, that remained shut like the cold room had, a science experiment, one of the many caves she set up just in case. I knew I could not do it, I couldn't walk into them and have them take me as I was, a tiny bird, a rush dweller, so I made do with gathering the blackberries into a bowl until Lila called me in, tidelike.

She poured sugar gently onto them and I went in and sat on the deep red brocade couch that had come with the house to listen to an old man tell the news. There were old men newsmen back then who you could not doubt. Dick was outside mowing the lawn. He had been in the front yard making a fool of himself with the electric mower cord and was in the side yard now with the bright yellow forsythia, which I had never liked even though I knew I should, but I did like it because Lila liked it.

I looked over at her through the doorway of the kitchen past the kitchen table in front of the stove and my mind filled in that she was stirring something slowly. I watched the old man with his white hair's mouth bob and the sound of the mower made it harder for a second or so to hear so I looked back over and saw Lila darting from the dish drainer to the kitchen table to slam a tall shiny knife through the tablecloth into its fibers. She ran past me to the edge of the front part of the living room and turned on the record player, apologizing to me but still insisting on putting on the LP "Cats." She turned it up louder than the mower, scuttled over to the bureau like the land crab I remember seeing in the parking lot of Tom Thumb the day Dick had gone in to sell his first vile of mace when he was a salesman in the Keys and starting singing "Memory." She was balling, bursting with song, ladling it out for certainly me, certainly Dick, and certainly the neighbors on either side to hear, crying as though I had just died, one would think, and I watched Les Charles, the anchorman, the old, stoic anchorman, went into his soul for a second through the TV glass, forgot my mom, meditated, as it were, up until Dick was there on the disgusting bamboo chair holding her, she resisting, but being the straightjacket she had ordered.

This morning, the morning before all memory, she is in bed in the living room, what the room became when she got too sick to get up anymore. On Saturdays I used to sit on the back of the brocade couch where I used to watch the Smurfs, the exact place where I got my first headache and experienced the relief of my first Tylenol, and watch all the cartoons I could think of with my mother cooking in the kitchen next to me, the windows open sometimes, often rain fogging up the windows and becoming a reason in of itself to love each other. This morning she isn't there and I am not, I got up late because I could feel her not awake, not "to," and I lay in bed wondering if there was some way to make the window in my room not feel like that, not feel sad, feel sunny again, feel like the window to the outside, not just another picture on the wall.

Lila had been cut apart from herself when she was still unable to dress, when Ada still called to her that her bath was ready. She had a porcelain face with dark doll hair and wore layered dresses until she was 15 when she got to choose boys shorts and blue Keds with no comments from her lanky Ford model mother who had gone to UCLA and her father, the cross-dresser doctor; there was nothing wrong with that.

Her mother, her. There was no talking, no reasoning, just the heights. Never descending because valleys were clouded by the eternal force in her glass, tinkling around everything. Never would you think such a delightful sound could be so sinister. Tiny Lila never had a moment to relax. Ada tended her like a horse but without blood to do those things there is something missing. The ones who shared it were all like her mother and that's what she became too, a pause, the sound in between beats that cocks your ears in anticipation, the breath before a laugh.

The thing that was most different about Lila was there was no tinkling or fancy dresses, except the Jessica McClintocks Big Mama's daughter would send that I would scale the metal fence in to grab a quick glass of milk or the hors d'oevres Lila would make for me and my friends. You can take the debutante out of the ball, but you can't take the ball out of the debutante, it seemed. Our house in the old city was damp and sombre with pictures torn from art books of the Virgin Mary and streaks of mutterings on the walls melted there by her eternal frying and boiling. After Edward left the island we headed for was small, the cabin was small, there were bunk beds and faux wood and the reason for the lack of tinkling was Lila drank beer from a can. Cockroaches crawled in, and everything absurd was funny. We were teenagers, all of us. But I only wanted to learn how to talk to the bunnies and land crabs and learn who all the fishes were and the great white heron who came to visit while I was fishing and Lila sunning on the little white rocks. I woke each day hoping and for years not even penetrated by the typing and the memories of tinkling and the deep imprint of sorrow in her face.

I don't like to talk about Dick. I feel he has been drawn badly by Lila and he had a hard start because he came into my room while I was being alone with my tornado cellar thoughts and I had to stand by the mirror while he asked me ceaselessly if I would simply respond to him, in any fashion, preferably hello. He became a part of her, washed asunder by her tide, only to surface through stories of Norway and the conquerors, and his quintessential childhood, an upbringing thrown off by beauty.

He was the umpire, then the tour guide, the sense

of reason, then the other voice in the hallway outside the bathroom. The Easter Bunny tooth fairy and finally the man on the couch, waiting to be escorted out by a teenage girl who had never learned to respect adults lying to themselves (sense of decency). For years I went again to the small Fishing and Hunting publishing building where I would check on him, see the photograph of Lila covered in a fishing vest and know that he was ruined, grab 20 dollars and build on my growing sense of relief that I was not and would never be that, whatever it was, that carried the past around not only not so obviously but at all.

In the ancient summer day he held her like a rock in his hand until she went back into the kitchen to make gumbo. That tiny thread like the rope around a boat edge had been bitten off when she was a small puff of steam. Everything was painted that way.

The morning of I came into the living room where my mother lay sunken into the waterbed, Saltines and beer next to her, the bent 1960s blinds drawn to cover the daylight.

"Can I watch cartoons? The dishes are done. The Smurfs are on. Fat Albert is almost over ..."

She feigned sleep or at least a daze. I walked back into the kitchen. I looked for a moment at the neat array of dishes in the dish drainer, wondering if I had put them in there in the right order, as an adult might have done. I removed the step stool, placing it under the sink, leaving the white washed kitchen washed in bathing daylight, the green flecked tile floor remembering me, remembering me to myself, and went into my room to play the flute. I left the door open a crack that I might not be trapped within my own room, or have a garden without light or appetite.

About the Author

Cristen Hemingway Jaynes was born in Seattle, Washington, but spent much of her youth traveling across the country with her author mother, Lorian Hemingway. They spent most of their summers in the Florida Keys. As an adult, Cristen continued their tradition of exploring the United States, making many trips across the country by bus and train. Cristen credits these wanderings with giving her the material for her stories. She has spent the past three years in New York City, working on her forthcoming collection, Dragonflies.

www.cristenhemingwayjaynes.com

Made in the USA
Charleston, SC
09 May 2016